Married to the Outfit

Mabel Lang

Contents

1

Chapter 1

New Orleans

2016

Streaks of the pale crescent moon illuminated the balcony of the Italianate mansion. On it, sat the oldest and only daughter of The Family's underboss. The detailed iron wrought balcony almost acted as a frame capturing Nina's allure as she leaned against it. A smile played on her lips as a million chirping crickets greeted her ears and the humid air caressed her olive skin. Everything felt serene and made her fall into a state of daydreaming.

One that she got quickly ripped out of as she felt someone's hand on her arm. She quickly spun around and was met with the smiling figure that was her brother.

"I knew I'd find you here."

She shook her head at him and released a gentle laugh. "You have to stop sneaking up on me like that, Giorgio."

"I'm not doing it on purpose – cross my heart." He grinned. "Just so you know, Mom is looking for you."

"I know she is."

After a light chuckle, Giorgio's cheerfulness slowly disappeared behind a sombre expression. He had come on their mother's behalf, believing it would soften the blow if he delivered the card in his hand rather than her.

"Here" – he handed her a decorated card – "it's your uh- or I guess I don't have to explain."

Melancholy writ on Nina's face as she looked at the wedding card. It looked beautiful. The laser-cut lace pattern was moved to the side, making it possible to read the bride and groom's name in black ink. She let her fingers softly touch the cotton fiber, wanting to burn it to a cinder.

In the past, Nina always expected she would be married off to someone from her hometown. In that scenario, she would still be close by to the few people she cared about. But after being told she was to marry the future Don of The Chicago Outfit, that idea got quickly shoved out of her head.

"What do you think? I picked it out." She asked him about the design of the card. It was one of the few things she had a say in.

"I hate it."

A burst of laughter came out of Nina and when she quieted down, she agreed with him.

Giorgio continued saying, "The Family can do without their help."

"Giorgio," she said with a sigh. "You know nothing."

"Yes, I do," he mumbled as his brown eyebrows knitted together.

"The Family can't keep fighting a war on three fronts." Nina held his arm, giving it a squeeze. "It's you who is going to be on the front line and if marrying Luciano brings three down to two then I'll gladly do it."

"I can try to talk Dad out of it."

"As if I haven't tried that already. And what makes you think he will change his mind now?"

"Maybe he'll listen to me."

Bitterness crept into her being like poison. "We both know he won't. He's incapable of doing that kind of thing," she said knowing how prideful her father was. Noticing how her breaths had become shorter she told her brother he could find her in the garden.

Nina often sought shelter in her most beloved place in the house whenever she got a reminder of reality. Lately, her mother had been the cause of that. She had been getting more and more urged on to perfect her future duties as an Italian wife. A duty she had managed to escape up until now.

Nina walked under the wooden arches in the garden, the white gardenias surrounding her. A silvery glow kissed the blossomed flowers and made her lightly graze its petals. She took a deep breath in and out. The velvety scent floated throughout the air having a calming effect causing her lips to tip up again.

"There you are, Nina! I've been looking everywhere for you!" her mother shouted from the upper balcony, sounding exasperated.

"Giorgio already delivered the card." Nina continued walking the other way, not being able to take her seriously.

Only when she heard the booming sound of her father's voice slicing through the air, her legs had come to a halt and stood in the middle of the paved path. He had called her name. Nina's smile faded, a questioning gaze taking its place. She faced the other way and saw her father standing at the end of the tunnel archway.

"Give the girl some space, Evelyn. You're going to give her a headache like this," Carlos said to his wife.

Nina headed in her father's way wondering why he had come to her. As far as she was concerned, she hadn't broken any of the unwritten rules. Getting in trouble was a foreign concept.

Despite that what she knew, it didn't stop her usual calm from slipping away. The roaring sound of her heartbeat didn't settle down and it only seemed to get louder with each footstep.

When the two met in the middle, Nina regarded the expression he wore. If it was an indication for anything, she seemed to have good news waiting for her.

"Yes, Papà?"

"You'll get to meet him on Friday." Carlos lifted his arm toward the paved path, suggesting they would go for a stroll.

Nina was a few steps behind her father as she tried to make sense of his words. Slowly but surely, it dawned upon her who he was referring to. Never before had something like this happened.

He continued saying, "If you'll be your usual self, everything will go smoothly. You already know but don't say anything unnecessary."

His words made her heart sank to the bottom of the cold ocean. Often enough, he would lightly throw around these kinds of re-marks.

Nina made fists out of her hands. "Like my opinion on this arrangement?"

Carlos threw his head back in laughter. "Exactly. I don't think those men in Chicago would know what to do with a woman with a brain."

Neither do you.

"Is there really no one else who can marry him?" her voice crack-ing under pressure. This was her last chance to try and change her father's mind. Her last chance to change her sealed fate.

Carlos came to a stop and looked over his shoulder before fully turning around. The hard set of his jaw told Nina she was in a losing battle. "Are you still going on about that?" his voice was stern, leaving no place for any further disagreement.

"Of course, I am! How can you expect me t-" Nina was cut off by the sudden force on her cheek.

Nina was taken aback by her father's action. In comparison to her little brother, she could still count the number of times he had hit her on her fingers. Carlos was usually more lenient toward his daughter than his son, but on this particular day, he wasn't. He was finally so close to getting what he wanted.

"I will hear no more. You will do as you are supposed to. You're no exception to the rules in our world."

Nina held her hand against the red cheek as she watched her father step closer to give a hug. She rested her stinging cheek against his shoulder. It didn't come as a surprise, he often embraced her right after hitting her. Nina never knew whether he did it because he regretted hitting her in the first place or if this was his way of consoling her.

"You're strong, Nina. I know you can do this for The Family."

"Papà-

"Don't." The amount of pressure Carlos put on his teeth caused one to believed they would crack and pulverize. "No matter how many times we have this conversation, it always ends the same way."

"Is there anything else you wanted to tell me?"

Her obedient tone led him to relax his body. Carlos let go of her, took a step back and stroked his daughter's dark-brown hair. "Tell your mother so she'll know to buy ingredients for dinner. It's not just Luciano who'll be coming. Their consigliere is also coming. Everything has to be top-notch."

Nina only nodded, left the garden and set foot in the house. Only when she was engulfed by the shadows in the hallway, she let a few stray tears fall. Nina wiped them off with the fabric of her long sleeves. She quickly looked up when she saw a shadow nearing her.

"You look a little down. Is it because of the card?" Giorgio said.

Nina shook her head dismissively and asked where their mother was.

"In the kitchen. She said she had something in the oven."

Nina made her way down the hall toward the kitchen and found her mother humming happily to a song playing on the radio. She never seemed to take notice of everything happening around her – unless it was something scandalous.

"Papà wants you to go to the French Market," she said, making her mother place the folded dishtowel on the counter beside her. "Luciano and someone else are coming over on Friday."

Her mother gasped. Nina couldn't make out if she was happy or shocked hearing the news. On one hand, her mother had little to no time to prepare everything and on the other, this meant her daughter would finally get an engagement ring. The agreement between the Sciacca and the Gallucci family would be official at last. Nina was well aware of how her mother cared about the opinions of other people in their circles. To finally have her only daughter be engaged was an affair of huge significance. An unmarried daughter would be no good.

"You don't have to worry about anything, Nina. I'll make sure everything is perfect!"

Nina didn't say anything in return and instead climbed the stairs. She leaned against her bedroom door and slid to the floor. A strange sense of calm washing over her as she stared at the floor.

Deep down, Nina believed her father was right. This was the world they lived in and she was no exception. This was their normal. She would have to do her part just like those who came before her.

2

CHAPTER 2

Time seemed to fly by in Nina's mind. Before she knew it, it was Friday. The day Luciano would come. Nerves seeped into her being like poison. All of the collected calm she had in the past few days went flying out the window.

She had her hair in an updo, a few locks falling to the sides of her face. Nina chose to wear a Bordeaux floor-length dress with slits, showing off her smooth long legs.

"This stupid thing is not working with me!" Giorgio grumbled as he barged into his sister's room.

"And a little privacy would be nice," Nina said and looked at the crumpled up tie in her brother's hand. "Here, let me do it." She held her hand out.

Nina got the black tie handed over to her and helped her brother out. After she was done, she smoothed it over with her hand. Nina never said it out loud, but she liked having her little brother rely on her from time to time. Even if it was for small things like this. In the eyes of the family, Giorgio was a made man but to Nina, he was still her beloved brother.

"You know, you should really learn how to do it on your own."

"I don't have to when you're here." He gave her a cheeky smile making her laugh as well.

"Not for long anymore." Nina sobered up at her realization.

I'll be in Chicago. Away from my family and surrounded by new people. Nobody to rely on or ask for help. Papà and Giorgio won't be able to help even if I wanted them to. I'll be under the rule of the Gallucci. Under Luciano's iron fist.

Giorgio saw the unease her eyes reflected. "Don't worry. Those fuckers have no power here. I'll let them know they don't own the place."

Nina shot Giorgio a disapproving look. "Please, Giorgio don't say anything rash. I don't want to start on the wrong foot with him."

"You're serious, aren't you?" He sighed and continued, "I'll try to be on my best behaviour."

Nina smiled and even though she knew he would only do the bare minimum, she appreciated the effort. With her brother leaving the bedroom, her mother entered. She let her know of the arrival of their guests and left again.

"He's here already." Nina let out a shaky breath.

It's fine. I'll be fine. Stay calm. Nina assured herself. Her hands on her chest, trying to keep herself from panicking. I can do this. She threw her shoulders back, keeping a straight posture and her head held high.

She turned the lights of her room off, closed the door and descended the stairs. It was faint but she could hear the sound of people talking in the foyer. One of them was clearly her father but the other two were unknown to her. Before letting her presence made known, Nina peered around the corner to see her fiancé.

Three men in suits. One with his back to her. Her father. The other two were faced in her direction. One slightly taller than the other, but both clearly above six feet. The first one to catch Nina's attention was the taller one of the two. He had pitch-black hair and an imposing look to him. The other man was a dark-blonde, his face veiled a sober look. Nina hoped the latter was her fiancé. Compared to the other one, the man with blonde hair appeared to be softer around the edges.

"What are you doing?" someone from behind said, startling her.

Nina quickly turned around to see the culprit. Her brother looked at her with a dumbfounded look on his face.

"Don't scare me like that."

"I didn't really mean to but sure."

It took Nina a few seconds to realise the talking of the other party had stopped. All eyes were now on the two siblings. Her father broke the silence by telling the two men, they were his children. Giorgio made his way over to the three men and Nina followed suit.

"What was that? I don't need to tell you to behave, do I?" Carlos said under his breath to Nina while Giorgio made his introduction.

Nina didn't miss the strain in her father's voice. She couldn't blame him. If possible, she too would have preferred their first impression of her to be better.

"I'm sorry, Papà," she said in a whisper.

When Giorgio was done introducing himself to the guests, Nina stepped forward. She began opening her mouth to introduce herself but her father beat her to it.

"My daughter, Nina. A beauty isn't she?" Carlos' chest puffed with pride.

I can speak for myself. Thank you, Papà. Nina sighed mentally.

"Certainly," the dark-haired man said with a polite smile and looked at Nina.

The blonde didn't say anything at all; going as far as avoiding eye contact with Nina.

I know I hoped for him to be my fiancé, but he can't even look at me. Do I look that bad? Or is he one of those arrogant types? Thinks he is better than women. Or does he just not want to be here?

Nina held out her hand to the man with dark blonde hair. "Nice to meet you. I'm Nina," she said with a sweet smile.

He shook her hand and said, "Nero."

Nina made a conscious effort to make sure her smile didn't falter. She diverted her eyes from Nero and focused on the daunting man next to him.

"Luciano?" Nina asked and shook his hand.

"Yes."

Nina made sure to meet his strong gaze. Now more than ever was she glad for the confidence she gained in the past two years. Back then, she would have been even more intimidated by the man in front of her.

"Well, let's not stand here all day," Carlos said.

Everyone moved away from the foyer and made their way into the spacious living room. With Luciano right behind her, Nina had to remind herself to breathe.

"If possible, I'd like a word alone with Nina," Luciano said to her father.

"Of course, first things first. You should do what you came here to do," Carlos replied and expectantly looked at his daughter.

Right. Nina mentally braced herself and turned around.

"I'm sure he can do whatever he wants right here," Giorgio commented and threw a hard look in Luciano's way.

"I could but I'd rather not."

In her head, Nina scolded her little brother. She was sure their father wouldn't give Giorgio's actions a pass. He would get punished for it. Usually, she liked her brother's protective side. Giorgio was never overbearing. In moments like these, she wished he thought about his own self-preservation.

"Will the garden do?" Nina suggested, hoping the outside air would help her cool down.

"Anywhere will do."

Definitely the garden.

The moment Nina set foot out of the house, she felt a little less tense. The uplifting flowers in the garden made her feel at ease.

Nina glanced at Luciano and took a moment to properly take in his defined features. The glimmer of the setting sun complimented his warm complexion. She was sure his piercing grey eyes often unsettled enemies and comrades alike. As if he could see right through them.

"Is your brother always like that? He should be more of aware his position. He is doing more harm than good."

His statement caught Nina off guard. She heard his warning loud and clear.

"He means no harm."

Luciano reached in the pocket of his black dress pants and took out a small velvet box. He opened it, revealing a ring. Golden band with a big diamond in the middle.

Most women would be thrilled to get such an expensive piece of jewellery. In Nina's eyes, the ring was anything but subtle. She guessed Luciano just bought whatever the jeweller recommend to him.

"Try it. See if the size is right."

Nina did as he told her to and put the engagement ring on her finger. It was a perfect fit. A while ago, her mother took a measure of Nina's ring finger and passed the info on to Luciano.

"It's lovely. Thank you," she said politely.

Voicing her actual opinion on the ring he chose for her seemed unwise. Refusing the ring would be seen as an act of defiance. She didn't want to be subjected to his wrath this early on in their relationship. She wanted to try and make it work. Nina saw Luciano narrowing his eyes at her. Gulping, she wondered if she said something wrong.

"What do you not like about it?" he asked. Still wearing the same grim look as before.

"It's very...," she stopped speaking, trying to think of the right word to use. "Let's say attention-grabbing."

The corner of his lip lifted as if she said something amusing to him. "I'll keep it in mind for your wedding ring."

Nina only nodded.

Can I hope for him to keep his word?

Nina's mind flashed to some of the horrid rumours she heard about Luciano. He was someone who had fallen from grace. Committing one crime after another. Nina didn't consider herself free from sin either. After all, she lived off the money made from similar crimes. Her engagement ring was a prime example of it.

"Was that all?"

"One more thing. The wedding ceremony will be in New Orleans but after we're done, we'll go straight to Chicago. You'll have to pack and send over the things you want to bring with you before that."

"I'll do that. Can we go back inside now? I'm starting to get a little cold." Nina made up an excuse, not wanting to be alone with Luciano for longer than she had to.

"On a summer evening?" He challenged her lie.

"I guess you are more accustomed to the cold than I am."

3

CHAPTER 3

Upon re-entering the house, Luciano joined the men sitting in the living room. Nina went the other way to help her mother out in the kitchen. Her mother, however, was already done. All that had to be done was set the table up for dinner.

"Is there something I can do?"

Evelyn waved her hand dismissively. "Never mind that. How did it go with him?"

Without realizing, Nina touched the ring Luciano gave her only moments ago. She wasn't sure how to answer. Her head was still too much in a state of chaos to make a full analysis on the brief meeting with her soon-to-be husband. Despite her inner turmoil, Nina made sure her outward appearance was flawless. To stay calm and collected. Elegant and graceful.

"Fine. It was fine." She showed her a quick smile.

Evelyn's gaze diverted to Nina's hand covering the shiny ring up. Rather abruptly, Evelyn took hold of her daughter's left hand. She was over the moon at the sight of the big diamond her daughter had gotten.

Nina always found her mother to a bit on the superficial side, but she understood where her mother came from. The gem she wore came with status and the size of it only amplified it. Her mother would be able to rub it in the faces of other salty women.

"Even your father didn't get me one like that when we got married. He is always so stingy. As if there is no extra money to spend," she huffed.

Nina ignored her mother's complaint and asked if anything of importance had happened in the meantime.

"I don't know how but by the grace of God your brother kept himself in check. But that's probably thanks to... what was his name again? The one with blonde hair?"

"Do you mean Nero?"

"Yes, him. He looks like a smart man. I don't think Giorgio will try to fight him. It's more Luciano and Giorgio I'm worried about."

Nina agreed. Judging from what she witnessed of their previous encounter, they were like water and oil. Having heard Luciano's criticism about her brother didn't appease her mind either. She was thankful they wouldn't be seeing much of each other in the future.

Evelyn grabbed the lasagne out of the oven and put it with the other dishes on the long table. Usually, she had the maids do the cooking in the house. Tonight, she wanted to impress her guests. When it came down to it, Evelyn made for a good host. While her daughter set the table up, she called the men for dinner.

Carlos was the last one to take his seat at the dining table. Nina settled in the chair between her mother and brother. Luciano and Nero sat opposite to them.

"Shall we say grace?" Carlos said as a kindly reminder making Giorgio place his silverware back on table.

Nina clasped her hands together whilst praying she was only imagining the expression on Giorgio's face. One that didn't bode well. Her brother looked like he wanted to call it a day. Nina could only hope for the rest of the evening to go without any more hitches.

Giorgio used to be someone who often sought out conflict. Once during a social gathering, Nina took the blame for his actions, resulting in people pointing an accusing finger at his sister. Ever since the incident, Giorgio wanted to be less like a little brother and more like a dependable older brother to Nina. Grow up for both their sakes.

"I won't try anything, so you can stop looking at me every second," Nina heard her brother say quietly.

She hadn't realised what she was doing until her brother pointed it out.

I must have looked really antsy if Giorgio could see it as well. I need to hold out a little longer. Tops an hour until they leave.

The voice of her mother brought Nina out of her thoughts.

"I hope you're enjoying your dinner."

"We are, Mrs. Sciacca," Luciano said politely and Nero nodded in agreement.

"Great and Nina is even better than me at cooking."

"I'm sure she is."

Luciano simply agreed with every praise Nina's parents made about her. Be it her natural beauty or her abilities to do wonders in the kitchen. Had he not done so, it would've resulted in his soon-to-be in-laws getting bitter feelings.

Nina could suddenly feel a shiver run down her spine. Without a doubt, she knew it was Luciano who had settled his eyes on her. She deliberated on what she should do. Ignore it or face it. Doing what she did best, Nina returned Luciano's attention with a gentle smile.

A thin layer of amusement covered Luciano's features before breaking his gaze away.

The only background noise in the room was Nina's mother speaking about the upcoming wedding in two months. All of it fell on deaf ears. In her opinion, her mother spoke far too often about the topic. Nina didn't need to hear more of it than she already had.

"And what about you? Are you already married?" Evelyn looked curiously at Nero.

"I'm not, Mrs. Sciacca."

"Now, that is odd. Why would a young man such as yourself still be single?"

Nina regarded Nero's subtle change in posture. A little straighter, a little bit more closed off. His hands gripping the silverware with more force and the tips of his ears became a shade of red.

Oh, no. Is he getting angry? He does look like a private man and I think I can say the same about Luciano.

"There's no particular reason," Nero said.

The only surprising thing during the rest of dinner was her father's watchful eye on her. Everybody knew Nina wouldn't stray from the rules set on her but her father wanted to be on the safe side. His usual trust in her obedience was gone. It made Nina re-evaluate the importance of the truce between the Sciacca and the Gallucci family. She couldn't allow herself any mistakes.

When everyone was done, they gathered in the foyer. From beginning to end, the men from Chicago kept up their formal attitude. When it was time for Nina to say her farewell to Luciano, she excepted a simple handshake as he had done a few hours ago. Instead, Luciano brought Nina's hand to his lips, kissing it right above the gold decorating her finger. The act took her by surprise. On the outside, she showed no reaction whatsoever.

She noted the slight twitch under his eyes, his expression bearing some semblance to fascination.

After the men from Chicago left the home of the Sciaccas, Nina took a deep breath. This would be the first and only time they met until the fated day. Next time she would see Luciano would be at the altar.

Carlos didn't delay his chance to discipline Giorgio. His son didn't try defending himself against the brute force he used on him. His daughter didn't seem to agree with his methods.

"Papà, he was just trying to-"

"Not a word, Nina," he raised the volume of his voice and turned his attention to Giorgio again. "You think that because I'm your father everything will always work out. That you can do whatever you want! You're too much like your mother's old-self," he muttered the last part bitterly.

Nina was surprised at the last piece of information. She had no idea what her mother was like in her younger days. Nina glanced at her mother who looked downward.

"I'll have a talk with your uncle and have you work under your cousin from now on. He isn't as forgiving to his soldiers as I am," Carlos said to Giorgio and left.

Her mother followed after him. Nina assumed she was going to try and ease his annoyance. Keep him happy by recounting the good things that happened tonight.

"Are you alright?" Nina said.

Giorgio laughed before quieting down, "I'm not the one you should be worried about, Nina. Dad isn't exactly wrong. What about you?"

"Nothing I can't handle." She reassured her brother and herself.

"If you say so."

Even her own brother was not privileged to seeing her drop the strong front she put up.

Nina went to the kitchen to lend her mother a helping hand with cleaning up. Her father who was also present took this as his moment to leave and stalked off. There was no denying the heavy air hanging around them.

They fought again.

She felt bad for her mother and gave her a hug. It lasted a few seconds before they pulled away from each other.

"Here, let me help you."

Evelyn refused her help. Explaining she wanted to keep herself busy. Keep her mind from going toward a vicious downward spiral.

"Go and get some rest, Nina. You must be tired."

Nina obliged and made her way to her bedroom. At last, she had a moment alone. A moment where she wasn't constantly being watched. The only place where she felt like she didn't have to look put together.

She stood in front of the leaning mirror and pulled every hairpin out of her updo, letting her hair fall to her mid-back. Nina slipped out of the dress, quickly got in her sleepwear and sank into the pillows on the bed. She stretched her left arm out and beheld Luciano's mark of rule on her.

In moments like this, Nina wished there was someone she could pour her heart out to. Someone she could emotionally rely on.

4

CHAPTER 4

A week had passed by since the men from The Outfit came to New Orleans. Life in the city became tranquil again due to a momentary stop in the feud between the Italians and the Irish. With the Irish pulling back and biding their time, business was going strong for the New Orleans family.

The Sciacca household was relatively quiet. The only ones present in the house were Carlos, Nina, the maids, and the guards who were on their posts outside.

Nina was early up to water the roses in the garden. A little earlier, her mother asked her if she wanted to go to Canal Place with her but she declined the offer. Shopping and gossiping about other women in their community went hand in hand. If given the opportunity, Nina would rather avoid indulging in those activities.

After she was done watering the other beds of flowers, Nina took a moment to relish in the warmth of the sunlight hitting her face.

The crashing sound of glass snapped her back into reality. Dark eyebrows drew together in confusion. Nina stepped inside to find the source of the noise. First, she checked the living room, then the kitchen and asked the working maids what had happened.

"We don't know, Ms. Sciacca. It came from upstairs."

Nina left the maids to their work and climbed the stairwell up. Reaching the top, she heard muffled voices coming from her father's working space. The wooden door got opened and she came face to face with her father.

"Oh, you're already here. Come inside," Carlos said and walked right back into his study, leaving the door open for his daughter to enter.

Her eyes immediately settled on the other man in the room. Her uncle and also the boss of the New Orleans family. Nina could only describe him as an unpleasant man.

Similar to her father, her uncle had dark-brown hair. Both were about the same height. The most distinct feature on her uncle's face was the drooping of his right upper eyelid. He sustained it after getting a stroke a few years ago.

"Good morning, Uncle Galasso." She forced a smile.

"Yes, good morning."

Her eyes wandered around the room and found a sea of tiny crystal-like pieces on the floor. Three of the five glass shelves were completely shattered.

Why is he even here? Did they get into a fight?

She examined the hands of her father and uncle from afar. Both seemed unharmed and there was not a single drop of blood in sight. Just like the men, Nina opted for standing instead of sitting down as usually was done when summoned into the study.

"I'm afraid I'll be the bearer of bad news today," her uncle said.

You always are. Nina wanted to say it out loud but didn't. She knew better than to anger the boss of the family.

Bad news? I don't know if I want to hear any bad news today and since they're telling me, I'm going to be shocked if this isn't about Luciano.

"Your wedding will have to be postponed."

Nina wasn't able to hide the surprise in her face. In her eyes, the revelation was anything but bad news. She knew the wedding was inevitable but being able to stay with her family for a little longer was a small victory.

That explains the glass. I'm just glad I wasn't here when Uncle Galasso broke the news to Papà. I can't imagine him being in high spirits.

"When is it now?" she looked at her uncle.

"The original date has been set back by two years, Nina."

I'll be twenty then.

"Unbelievable," her father muttered angrily. "That was all, Nina. You can go."

Nina nodded in response. She needed someone to talk to and asked her father if she could go to her aunt Noemi.

"Yes, but don't forget to bring a guard with you and before you leave call one of the maids. Tell them to clean this up." He motioned his hand in the general direction of the broken glass.

"Yes, Papà," she said and left to get one of the maids in the kitchen.

Upon entering the kitchen, the maids went silent. A few murmurs here and there. Nina knew they were gossiping about her family, but she wasn't going to scold them for it. After all, the maids' whispers were one of the few resources of information Nina got.

Nina might not participate in gossip but she certainly didn't ignore it either.

"My father needs someone to clean the glass in his study."

"I'm on it, Ms. Sciacca," one of the younger maids said and scurried away.

In the foyer, Nina wore her coat, stepped outside and called the guard near the entrance of the house to her. She made her request to the man who was her shadow and drove to her aunt.

Most members of the Sciacca family lived relatively near each other. The only one who didn't was her aunt Noemi. While it was never said out loud, it was because of her husband. A man the Sciaccas weren't all too keen on.

While Nina did ask her father to go to her aunt, it was really her cousin she wanted to see. Nina viewed her more like a little sister than anything else. She was three years younger than Nina. In the past, the two girls would often sleep over at each other's place. More often at Nina's home than her cousin's.

"Do you need me to stay put, Ms. Sciacca?" her guard Orlando asked when they arrived.

She shook her head. "No, you can go back. I don't know how long I'm staying so I'll call you later."

As she crossed the street, Nina noticed a familiar black car with two men sitting in it. They were either NOPD detectives or FBI agents. Officials were still under the impression that the Espositos were a big fish in the New Orleans Family.

Not paying any heed to them, Nina greeted the guard in front of her aunt's house and pressed on the doorbell. The door swung open, revealing a woman shorter than herself. Her aunt aged like fine wine. Still the same beauty she was in her younger days.

"Morning!" Nina smiled and copied her aunt by giving a kiss on the cheeks.

"Nina! Sweetheart, hurry up, come in!"

"What do I smell?" She raised a brow. The moment Nina stepped inside the house, she got a whiff of cinnamon.

Noemi let out an embarrassed laugh. "I tried this new cake recipe but I put too much cinnamon in it. Blame it on my love for the spice. I can't get enough of it."

Nina laughed for the first time in a while. The bright personality of her aunt never managed to let her down. Nina looked up at Noemi, she always thought of her as a strong woman.

"By the way, Rosaria is in here room, Sweetheart. I'll go check up on my cake."

Nina made her way to her cousin. She knew the inside of the house like the back of her hand. Before entering Rosaria's room, she knocked softly against the white door and pushed it.

"Nina!" A big smile broke out on Rosaria's face as she rushed over to give Nina a hug. "I missed you so much. I haven't seen you in so long!"

"I missed you too, Rosy!"

Nina shut the door and joined her cousin. They sat on a fluffy carpet and leaned against the frame of the bed.

"Your mother seems to be in a good mood. Is your father away?" Nina said.

"Thank God, yes. I've been avoiding my father but I overheard him telling Mamma he had to go to Uncle Galasso his place."

Nina's eyebrows were knitted after hearing Rosaria. "Uncle Galasso? That can't be true. He is with my father now. They are at my house and I didn't see your father when I left."

Rosaria shrugged. "Well, I don't care either way. As long as he is away from here."

Nina had a pretty good guess where Rosaria's father was. Having a mistress was a common practice for men. At least it was for the men in The New Orleans Family. The women were expected to be faithful while the men could stroll around and do as they pleased.

There wasn't a shadow of doubt in Nina's mind, her aunt thought of her husband's infidelity as a blessing in disguise. After all, Noemi's husband was almost twenty years her senior.

"But why was Uncle Galasso at your place?"

Nina took a deep inhale, "About that...the wedding is going to be postponed for another two years."

Rosaria's jaw dropped to the floor. "Really? That's amazing, Nina! I don't want them taking you from me. But why? What happened?"

Nina momentarily froze. She hadn't even thought to ask her father why it wasn't going through.

"I don't know."

"You don't? Nevermind that, what was meeting your fiancé like? What does he look like? How old is he even? And does-"

Nina held her hand over her cousin's mouth to stop her from asking a million questions at once and laughed. "Take it easy, Rosy."

Her cousin showed a meek smile until her eyes fell on the engagement ring. "You're kidding me. Did he give this to you? Don't get me wrong, I'm sure it's worth a lot but it isn't you."

"Yes, and really it's fine. I'm not too big on it either."

"So, your fiancé?" Her cousin urged her to tell her more.

"I wasn't alone with Luciano for long so I can't really say. He's handsome but that doesn't really matter when he's as intimidating as a person could possibly be. As for his age, Luciano is twenty-five but I'm pretty sure his birthday is coming up, so it might as well be twenty-six."

"So a seven-year difference. I mean look at the bright side, it's not some old wrinkly man you're getting," Rosaria unintentionally made light out of Nina's situation. "Wait, I don't mean it like-"

"No, I get it. You don't have to start walking around eggshells with me, Rosy." Nina held her cousin's hand to reassure her.

"For once, I'm glad we're the black sheep in the family. I haven't gotten any proposals coming my way. Thank God, I haven't. My father has been asking and looking around for someone though. He said and I quote 'I need to get you engaged before it's too late. Nobody will want you after you're twenty, Rosaria.' The nerve he has to say that." Rosaria huffed.

"Don't listen to your father."

Nina and Rosaria continued chatting for the rest of the day. She stayed around for dinner and ate with her aunt and cousin. Glad, her uncle didn't come home to eat with his family. Much like Noemi and Rosaria, Nina didn't want him around either.

"This is the best," Rosaria said as she munched on her banana foster.

Nina hummed in agreement. "It's childhood."

Noemi's eyes lit up at Nina's words. "It really is."

After giving her guard a call to come and pick her up, Nina helped with cleaning up. Just as they finished washing all the dishes, her guard arrived.

"Wait! Take this with you." Noemi handed Nina a container filled with cinnamon cake.

Her heart melted at her sweet aunt. "Thank you, Aunt Noemi."

Nina said her goodbyes and left with her guard Orlando to her house. She put the plastic box on her lap and watched the blurry streets as they passed them. Nina pondered over the question her cousin asked.

Why was it postponed? I can't believe I didn't even ask. I could try and ask Papà tomorrow but I doubt he'll give me a real answer. Maybe Uncle Galasso? Were they even told the reason by the people from Chicago? I know there is a truce between our families but it's not as if we are that close to disclose sensitive information to each other.

By the time they got to her home, forty minutes had passed. The sky dark and the streetlamps illuminating the pavement. She took note of the cars outside the house. Everybody was already home, except for her. She got inside and went straight to the kitchen to put the cake there.

"What do you have there?" Giorgio asked over his shoulder.

"Cake. Aunt Noemi made it. Do you want some?"

"Sure. Why not?" he said casually.

Nina knew her brother was downplaying how much he wanted the treat. He had a sweet tooth like no other. She sliced a piece for herself and one for her brother.

"How was your day?"

"Fine but don't cross paths with Dad in the next few days. His fuse is too damn short," Giorgio grumbled.

Everything considered, Nina thought her father's mood would be worse. She half-expected to see broken furniture lying around when she came home.

"Why does that not faze me?"

5

CHAPTER 5

The previous night, Nina kept fiddling with the gold adorning her ring finger. Her thoughts about Luciano keeping her awake. She needed answers to her questions.

Nina woke up with a drawn-out yawn. If possible she'd stay in bed a little longer but problems weren't going to fix themselves. She got up and took a shower in the bathroom attached to the bedroom. She styled her hair in a neat high ponytail and had casual formal wear on her body. Always making sure to look well-groomed even if she was only around family.

Nina made a bee-line for her father's workroom. Instead of making her presence known, she listened carefully if her father had any guests like yesterday. There wasn't any conversation to be heard. She threw her shoulders back and lifted her head before tapping against the door.

"Who is it?"

"It's me."

Carlos recognized his daughter's voice and said, "You can enter."

Nina walked inside and stood by the door. She hoped for this to be a quick visit. Her brother already informed her about their father's temper. Putting as much space as possible between herself and her father was the best thing she could do.

"What do you want?" his tone was clipped. Carlos' eyes were glued to the paper files on his desk. Not sparing a single look at Nina.

"You and Uncle Galasso never told me why the wedding is going to be at a later date."

A gloom fell over his facial expression. The word 'wedding' had apparently become a taboo word. A harsh breath came out of his mouth as he intertwined his fingers. He tried to keep an outburst at bay.

"There is no need for you to know. The only thing that matters is that in a year and three months, you'll be married and Chicago and New Orleans can finally move on and start working together." Carlos lifted his gaze and shook his head in disappointment when he realised what his daughter planned on doing. "If I'm not answering you, you sure as hell can forget your uncle will. Not that it matters since he is out of town."

Nina mentally laughed at herself. What did I think to come here? Did I really think Papà would tell me?

"I thought you had grown up, but you're still naive. Don't be like that in Chicago. They won't like women who meddle too much in business." It was Carlos' way of looking out for his daughter.

Her father's comment on her personality was inaccurate. Nina was more hopeful than anything else. She knew what the men around her were like, but she still had a sliver of hope in her that there were exceptions.

A feeling of resignation filled her as she walked out of the room. The boss and underboss of the family weren't going to tell her anything. The next best person Nina could go to was the consigliere. A man who had a critical role when it came to making important decisions concerning the well-being of the family. Nina halted when she realised she had no way of contacting her uncle's advisor.

"What are you doing?" Giorgio tilted his head.

"Nothing really. What about you?"

"I'm going out. Arturo called me in," he said making Nina hum with mild interest.

The two siblings walked beside each other toward the stairs. An idea popped in Nina's head, making her stop in her tracks for the second time.

"On second thought, can I come with you? I need to speak to Arturo," she asked sweetly.

Arturo Sciacca was an older cousin of her. He was also the oldest son of her uncle Galasso. It wouldn't be a stretch for Nina to think her cousin might hold answers. There was a high chance her uncle let some information regarding her marriage slip around his son.

Giorgio shrugged his shoulders. "Sure, but I need to go right now. Are you ready?"

"Always." She smiled.

Before long, the two were on their way to Arturo's place.

"What do you need from cousin anyways?" Giorgio inquired as he navigated the road.

"I need to ask him something about the wedding."

Giorgio's muscles tensed by a fraction, his knuckles becoming white in the process. He found the unity between the two families to be a good thing but wished it wasn't at the expense of his sister.

"If I could have done something to prevent it then I would have."

"Whatever you are doing, stop it. Don't beat yourself up over it." her tone stern. "It's not your fault."

"Fuck, Nina," he muttered. "I don't know what to do."

"What you need to do is stop looking at me and concentrate on driving."

"What if you got in a car accident and become crippled? They will cancel your wedding and give them another bride."

"Why didn't I think of that?" Nina feigned a pleasant voice. "Do you have any other bright ideas to tell me?"

"Sorry." Giorgio stayed quiet for a couple of seconds. "What if we had a different Don."

Nina stilled when she realised what her brother suggested. Her heart thumped loudly at the thought.

Kill Uncle Galasso? Is he losing his mind? I can't even tell how serious he is.

"Don't even joke about that, Giorgio."

"I'm not jo-"

"And don't ever speak like that around other made men," the sternness in her voice lost its balance and began to tremble. "God, Giorgio! You're going to get yourself killed like this. Promise not to do anything."

Giorgio groaned and pressed his lips together. "Cousin Arturo would be a better Don. He wouldn't have agreed to The Outfit's terms."

"But he isn't the Don, is he? This wistful thinking of you has to stop."

"Fine," he spoke as if the word was poisonous.

"And Giorgio-"

"Yes, yes, I promise not to get myself killed."

Soon enough, their trip came to an end and arrived at Arturo's doorstep. Giorgio knocked loudly on the entrance door. Waiting for their cousin to answer didn't take all too long. In front of Nina and Giorgio stood a tall brown-haired man with a manila folder in his hand.

"Nina?" Arturo's expression was stoic but his voice showed a hint of surprise.

"Hi, Arturo. Do you have some time?"

"Come inside." Arturo stepped aside to let Nina in. "Why don't you go to the living room? I need to speak to your brother. It won't take long, I'll be there in a minute."

Nina acted upon his request. She sat at the end of the light grey sofa and made herself comfortable. Her head rested against the palm of her hand and one leg was crossed over the other. Not much later, her cousin set foot in the room. Her brother not behind him and the folder he held just a few seconds ago gone.

"So, what brings you here?"

Nina noted his expression to be less stoic than before. The cause of it was his familiarity with her. Arturo knew her since she was little and therefore unintentionally lowered his guard around her. Usually, he was warier around others.

"Why was the date of the wedding set back?" She wasn't going to ease into the topic.

Arturo loosened his tie and sat on the armchair. "To be perfectly honest, nobody really knows."

His revelation made Nina frown. This wasn't the answer she was hoping to get.

"At least not the details of it. The Outfit only gave us a vague explanation. My best guess would be some kind of internal conflict. Their boss probably planned on handing the position down to Luciano after you married him. Which would mean a change in regime. It should come to no surprise if some of their members were opposed to having Luciano as their new leader."

"Why would they stand against Luciano?"

"Who knows? It could be anything. Maybe he has a few uncles or cousins thinking they're more entitled to the position than him. Things like this usually take years before fully resolved. You know how it is, Nina."

Nina nodded knowingly in response. "How long do you think it will take?"

"I don't know but it's likely most of it will be resolved before we unite. I hear the Gallucci rule with an iron hand. Especially, Luciano, he's ruthless."

Nina heard the same rumours about the Gallucci family. Slowly but surely, an anxious feeling inside her build up for what was to come.

Six months later

Evelyn had brought Nina to a chic bridal shop located in The French Quarter, wanting only the best for her daughter.

Nina sucked in her stomach as she tried getting into the white ball gown. This was one of the many wedding dresses she tried on. Outside the fitting room of the bridal shop waited Noemi and Rosaria who came for support.

"It's so tight, Mamma! I'm going to faint if I wear this," she groaned.

"Oh, stop exaggerating! You'll be fine. You look absolutely stunning. I knew we should've gone with the ball gown from the start. You're going to turn heads with this one."

"No, I'm not doing this. Can you get me the A-line dress you brought in earlier?" Nina gave an apologetic smile to the bridal consultant.

"Of course, Darling! I'll be back in a second." A wink was sent in Nina's way

She felt exhausted and wanted this day to be over with. The only one genuinely excited was her mother which was hardly a surprise for Nina. In the time the female worker was gone, Nina got out of the dress with the help of her mother.

Seemingly out of nowhere, Evelyn gasped and brought a hand on top of her mouth.

"I can't believe I forgot! Luciano's birthday already passed. We didn't even send anything."

The suspense left Nina's body after hearing what her mother had to say.

"It's fine, Mamma. I already took care of it."

A month ago, she wrote her fiancé a card and sent it along with a small present. He had turned twenty-six years old. She couldn't expect her marriage to go smoothly if she put no effort into it. Nina wanted to start on good terms with him.

The female worker came back with the A-line dress Nina wanted. She put it on and presented herself to Noemi and Rosaria.

"Good choice on the dress. You don't want to be walking in heels all day long and I would know." Noemi commented on the length of the dress as it flowed to the ground. "You look beautiful, Sweetheart."

In spite of the smile her aunt wore, Nina heard sadness dripping from the spilt words.

Rosaria nodded eagerly in agreement and looked her at cousin with awe. While Rosaria wasn't looking forward to Nina's wedding, she couldn't deny how the dress made her look ethereal.

Nina looked at herself in the long mirror. She tried to memorize the sight Luciano would see as she walked down the aisle.

A prideful and reputable bride.

The daughter of an underboss.

The niece of a don.

In a year and six months, she would no longer be under the protection of the Sciacca family but rather under that one of her husband.

6

CHAPTER 6

2018

Nina broke out in cold sweat as time ticked by. Today was the fated day that marked her to become part of the Gallucci family. It was almost time for her to stand at the altar.

She let her eyes wander down as she looked at the reflection of herself. Her snow-white wedding dress accentuating how pure she was. Her dark-brown hair in a low updo with the veil falling down from it and her ring matching with the bouquet she held. Nina placed her hand on her chest and tried to control her breathing.

It's fine. I'll be fine. I can do this.

Nina kept her feelings bottled up. She felt like collapsing and screaming from the top of her lungs but didn't. She couldn't. The young bride would do as she was expected to. She had a certain image of herself to keep up and it drained her energy.

"You look perfect, Nina." Her mother's eyes glistened with pride as she held onto her arm.

She forced the corners of her lips to tip up. "Thank you, Mamma."

"You're handling this so much better than I did on my wedding day." Evelyn let out a short laugh. "But you've always been so composed, mature and all. You're doing great. I'll go and get your father."

Nina was split in two listening to her mother. On one hand, she was glad there weren't any cracks to be seen in her mask. Her emotions weren't on her sleeves. On the other hand, no one knew what she was like on the inside. She never had a shoulder to cry on.

"Nina, look at me," her aunt Noemi said with a concerned look. "I get it. I understand."

Those simple words made tears well up in the bride's eyes. Noemi cupped her niece's face to stop her from crying.

Noemi continued, "I understand but I know you are strong. You have to believe in yourself and come out on top, Sweetheart."

Her aunt's words of encouragement meant more to Nina than she could've hoped for. Even if it was just a little bit, she felt the weight on her shoulders had become a tad lighter.

"You always know the right thing to say." Nina pulled her aunt in an embrace. This was the last bit of comfort Nina would get in a while.

"Noemi!"

Nina and her aunt turned to see who invited themselves in the room. It was her uncle by marriage, Rino Esposito, who came to get his wife. His arrival was unwelcome in Nina's mind. The old man would always look at her for much longer than was appropriate.

"What are you still doing here? I'm over there waiting, and here you are making me wait. We have to get to our seats. Now!" Rino snapped at his wife.

"I'm-"

Nina stopped her aunt from speaking further by squeezing her hand. "You need to go. I'll be fine. Papà will be here soon anyway."

Where her caring aunt once stood was now her father. He rubbed his hands together and had an eager look on his face. He waved her to come over, sparing no words. It was time for the ceremony to start.

Nina linked arms with Carlos and the two made their way toward the aisle. The moment the bride and her father entered, everyone stood up. The cathedral was packed with men, women and children from both families. New Orleans on the left side and Chicago on the right. On both sides, this union was the talk among people for a long time. Today, it was finally going to be realised.

Nina gulped as she felt all eyes on her. Curious, jealous and cold stares were fixed on the Sciacca bride. Therewas no avoiding the evil eye. Her pulse raced, yet, she still managed to walk gracefully down the aisle. Before she knew it, her father left her side and gave the flower bouquet to the maid of honour.

Luciano held out his hand for Nina which she obliged to take. She made sure her grip was firm enough to stop him from noticing her light shaking. Nina's composed appearance made Luciano look with intrigue at his bride.

The bishop began, "Dearly beloved, we are gathered here today to join this man and woman in holy matrimony."

Nina shifted her gaze from the priest to Luciano. A navy blue tuxedo and his hair styled back. The colour of his eyes were striking. He looked the same as he did when they first met, except for one subtle change. One naked to the eye if you looked at him from a distance.

The marriage officiant resumed his speech. Meanwhile, Nina re-focused on the scar above Luciano's left eyebrow that ran to his temple. Her gaze on him didn't go unnoticed. Nina's brown eyes met his dark grey ones, making her briefly look away.

Nina got a quick glance at the guests sitting on the front row. An elderly man with ash-grey hair and a cane beside him. He looked harmless, but Nina had no doubt he was the Don of The Chicago Outfit. Next to him sat a much younger person with black hair. His appearance was similar to Luciano's.

He does have a brother if I'm not mistaken.

The young man sent a wink in Nina's way. A bold action she didn't expect. In Nina's mind, no one in their right mind would risk behaving in a way that could be seen as flirting by others. The only person Nina knew was the man with dirty-blonde hair, Nero D'Angelo. The consigliere who had come to her home once before.

By the time Nina and Luciano had to exchange vows, an eery sense of calm swirled inside her. The bride and groom both came out with a strong and confident 'I do'.

"Repeat after me," the bishop said.

"I, Luciano Nicolò Gallucci, take you Nina Eleanora Sciacca to be my wife, to have and to hold from this day forward, for better, for worse, for richer, for poorer, in sickness and in health, to love and to cherish, till death do us part." Luciano's expression didn't reveal a single thing as to what he felt.

Nina did the same. "I, Nina Eleanora Sciacca, take you Luciano Nicolò Gallucci to be my husband, to have and to hold from this day forward, for better, for worse, for richer, for poorer, in sickness and in health, to love and to cherish, till death do us part."

The bishop asked the groom and bride to place a ring on each other's finger. Luciano first and Nina second. Nina's lips parted slightly at the golden ring Luciano got her. It had a small marquise cut diamond attached to it; nothing like the engagement ring he got her a year ago.

"By virtue of the authority vested in me under the laws of the State of Louisiana, I now pronounce you husband and wife. You may kiss the bride."

No matter how many times Nina told herself this would happen, it didn't stop the loud beating of her heart in her ears. All of her attention was on Luciano as if he was the only other person in the cathedral. After the removal of the veil, Nina felt his hands cupping her face and braced herself for what was to come. He showed no signs of going easy on her and went in for the kiss. Nina could feel herself flush under his touch.

"So far, this has been the only genuine reaction I've gotten out of you," Luciano said in a low voice so only she would hear him.

For a second, Nina could've sworn there was a hint of amusement to be seen in his expression. She didn't know how to respond to him and didn't get the time to do so as applauds erupted from the guests. The newlywed couple turned to face them. Nina showed them a courteous smile and Luciano a tight-lipped one. Nina looked over at her family and saw her parents' avid clapping, her brother who stared daggers at Luciano and her aunt Noemi and cousin Rosaria who only seemed to clap along because it was mandatory.

After all of the guests got out of the cathedral as tradition asked and stood right outside the building, Luciano and Nina followed. Luciano took hold of his wife's hand and walked down the aisle toward their families. The second the newlywed were out, confetti was sprinkled on them. It was supposed to signify the love and happiness between Nina and Luciano, but it was all a charade.

Who are they even trying to fool with this?

A little girl with wonder sparkling in her eyes drew Nina's attention. It looked as if the girl was seeing a fairy tale play out. Nina hadn't seen the girl's face before and guessed she was from the The Outfit.

Impressionable girls. I can't quite remember when I stopped being like that.

The bride's smile turned a bit more sincere as she waved at the girl and getting the same reaction in return.

Maybe things will be different in their city.

Right before Luciano and Nina parked a limousine that had white lilies decorating the hood. The vehicle would bring them to the hotel where the reception was going to be held.

With Luciano getting in from behind her, Nina changed positions. Her movement causing the satin of the dress to whisper against the leather. The enclosed space seemed much smaller with him right next to her.

Just as they slipped into traffic, her gaze glided from the road to Luciano; too aware she was alone with him.

"Do you have something to say?" Luciano felt Nina's eyes on him.

She shook her head. "No, nothing."

"You exceeded my expectations."

"Excuse me?" She furrowed her brows.

"I've been to a lot of weddings, but it's still rare to see a bride who doesn't look as if she's going to faint any minute. You won't, right, Nina? You'll stay as poised as ever, won't you?" His jaw tightened.

The piercing look in his eyes made Nina shudder.

"Do you not want me to be?"

"I do," Luciano said. "But not when you're with me."

7

CHAPTER 7

During most of the reception, Nina simply chose to be an observer at her own wedding. Watch from a distance how everything unfolded. All of the guests were well-behaved, except for one. A table or two away from the bride and groom, a young man caused a ruckus – a cousin of Luciano. He had one too many drinks and made a fool out of himself.

From the corner of her eyes, Nina saw the Chicago boss walk up to the young man. In her mind, he couldn't possibly think to lecture him in a place like that. Unsure of the Chicago boss' plans for the young man, Nina began reaching out to Luciano. She glanced at him but only see Luciano already watching the scene play out. Contentment shrouding his features.

What is Luciano's grandfather going to do? Please, don't let there be a fight.

The Chicago boss grabbed Luciano's cousin by his ear and pulled him to his feet. If it was anyone else doing it, it would be a clear sign of disrespect, but Luciano's cousin couldn't lift a finger to his boss. The young man was dragged out of the ballroom after the Don berated his grandson. Snickers rolled out from different corners of the grand room.

Nina immediately took note of the differences between the two families. In New Orleans, the defiant men got disciplined in private. There were several instances where this happened between Carlos and Giorgio Sciacca. In Chicago, however, another set of rules seemed to apply. Public humiliation was used as an effective tool for anyone who was out of line.

When it was time for the bride and groom to share their first dance, Nina swiftly closed her eyes. In addition to Luciano, she would also have to share a dance with her in-laws. All of them complete strangers to her.

Nina clasped hands with Luciano and the two proceeded to the dance floor. A slight hitch in Nina's breath as Luciano placed a possessive grip on her waist. She guessed it was to show everyone whose she was.

Throughout the remaining of their dance, Nina tried ignoring his burning gaze on her. She wanted him to look elsewhere. The scrutinizing looks from the people on the sides paled in comparison to Luciano's. Going by his words in the limousine, Nina believed he wanted to see behind the front she put up.

"You can't act as if I'm not here the whole time."

Nina turned slightly, their lips almost touching. "I'm not."

"If you say so." He sounded unconvinced.

"I'm trying to memorize all the new faces."

"You'll have more than enough time for that once we're back."

After the bride and groom were done, it was Carlos' turn to dance with his daughter. He reminded Nina of the duties she had to fulfil later on that night. The folks from the New Orleans family had a certain tradition that would take place on the wedding night. The husband had to take the virginity of his wife and present the tainted white sheets to the family as proof of consummating their marriage. Colour drained from Nina's face as she listened to her father. On the other side of the dancefloor were Luciano and his new mother-in-law sharing a silent dance. Friendly yet distant.

Nina's dance with her father only lasted a few minutes. In the eyes of the spectators, it was short and sweet. She was glad for it to be over.

"Can I have a dance with a bride as beautiful as yourself?" Nina heard a gruff voice say.

Alarms went off inside Nina at the sight of the Chicago Don. Since Luciano's father was no longer in the world of the living, his grandfather, Nicolò Gallucci, acted the role. Nina wouldn't let his charming smile lower her guard around him.

"I'd love to." She supplied with a sweet smile.

The elderly man handed his cane over to someone else when Nina accepted his request.

"You know, that smile of yours might work on everyone else, my grandson included, but not on me." At his old age, Nicolò Gallucci was still the same perceptive individual he always had been. "I can say with certainty, you'll make for a fine addition to the family."

"What makes you say that?" Nina had to be careful with her words. Technically, Don Nicolò was her boss now, rather than her uncle, Don Galasso.

"You're doing a good job keeping your act together."

Don Nicolò his words reminded Nina of what Luciano said to her earlier that day. In spite of that, there was a distinction to be made between the two. The former could see through Nina, while the latter wanted to, but couldn't.

Once Nina finished her dance with Luciano's grandfather, she thought of taking up a place in the background. A moment to slip away from the crowded ballroom and take a breather. A young man from the Gallucci family shattered her plan into little pieces by bringing the bride back to the dance floor. The man's name was Teodoro Gallucci, he was the younger brother of Luciano. Nina could hardly refuse his invitation because it would be seen as rude.

"Isn't this nice? We finally get to properly talk to each other," he said with a smile.

Up until now, Nina and Teodoro only got briefly introduced to each other by Luciano. She didn't take Teodoro to be that much older than herself. With Luciano still around, she made no mention of his brother's reckless deed during the wedding ceremony.

"What you did during the ceremony was inappropriate. People would think you were flirting." She referred to his wink. "And you're too close." Nina subtly placed a bit more distance between them.

He laughed. "Wouldn't that be a wonderful disaster? It would definitely make things more exciting."

"Are you always like this?"

In her head, Nina envisioned Luciano's brother to be somewhat similar to him. For now, she found their looks to be the only thing they held in common. Both had jet-black hair and the same grey colour in their eyes.

"No, but you cannot blame me for wanting to spice my brother's wedding up. Besides, I could ask you the same thing. You know, I wasn't sure what to think when I found out about Luciano's marriage but seeing you made me change my mind. My brother and you might be a match made in heaven."

This man. I don't even know how to deal with him. If there is anyone from Luciano's family I should get along with then it's his brother, but at this rate, it seems unlikely. Spice things up? What is he even going on about? A match made in heaven? Nina felt like pushing her brother-in-law to the ground and storming out of the ballroom. Stop it. He is just trying to rile me up. Get a reaction out of me. I guess he does share some qualities with Luciano.

Nina smiled kindly at Teodoro. "Well, you do know Luciano better than I do, so I'll take your word for it."

Later on, Nina managed to escape the ballroom and roamed the hollow hallways of the hotel. The bride was aware people would come looking for her. This moment of quiet was going to be short-lived. Nina thought back on the conversation she had with her father. She dreaded the bloody sheet tradition of her family.

"Are you okay?" someone grabbed her by the shoulder and made her turn.

Nina placed a hand on top of her heart. "You have to stop doing that."

"I swear to God, I'm not doing it on purpose," Giorgio said. "But are you okay?"'

"Yes. Who sent you to come and get me?"

"Who do you think? Dad," he drawled. "Also, Rosaria wanted to know how you were doing. She wanted to come with me to check up on you, but some random guy asked her to dance with him. You should've seen Uncle Rino's face, he looked like he could have died of happiness."

"Doesn't he always look like he's on the brink of death. That man is rotten in all kinds of ways."

Giorgio laughed. "That is true. I missed this part of you, Nina."

Her brother was one of few who got to hear Nina's unfiltered thoughts from time to time.

Giorgio took a good look at his sister. "I can't believe you won't be here tomorrow. The house will be different without you. I'll miss having you around."

"I'll miss you too." A genuine gentle smile formed on her lips. "I promise to call and visit as often as I can."

"When you come and visit, be sure to leave that husband of yours behind."

Nina gave her brother a look. "Don't ask the impossible of me. You know he'll come along. The best you can hope for is for Luciano to avoid you as much as you'll avoid him."

In close proximity to the Sciacca siblings were another two people occupying the hallways. Nina and Giorgio picked up a loud voice and headed in the direction where it came from. The closer Nina got the more distinguishable the male voices became. It was her father and her husband having a dispute. Nina stopped her brother from reaching the intersecting corridors, making sure they stayed out of sight from Carlos and Luciano.

Toward the end of their fight, Carlos' volume had raised a considerable amount. Luciano, on the contrary, kept his voice low and steady.

"You are forgetting I'm her husband now. You no longer hold any power over Nina," Luciano's tone was severe.

Carlos gritted his teeth. "That doesn't mean you can-"

"I do not want to keep repeating myself, Carlos. I've already decided what will happen. New Orleans doesn't have any say in the matter. My wife falls under the rules of the Gallucci. Not the Sciacca."

Nina couldn't figure out what their cryptic meeting was about. She regarded the way Luciano spoke to her father. While Luciano did not raise his voice against his father-in-law, it wasn't exactly the same polite tone he used before. Whatever Luciano decided on, Nina believed he had set his mind on it.

8

CHAPTER 8

Nina turned her head sideways before the heavy doors shut out the view of a whistling and cheering crowd. Most of them were men. She watched Luciano lock the door of the room they would spend their first night in.

Click.

Nina glanced around the room. Once again, avoiding his gaze on her and silently trying to avoid the inevitable. Her eyes stopped moving and settled on the bed. Just like her father told her, the milky-white sheets were there. She wanted to shred it to pieces and let flames consume it. Nina turned on her heel when she heard an unexpected sound come out of Luciano.

Does he think this is funny?

"Your family likes to test my patience, don't they?" He laughed under his breath.

While the corners of his lips were tipped up, his eyes didn't match it. Luciano wasn't humoured. The opposite seemed to be true.

Nina felt his arm brush against hers as he stalked past her, heading toward the large bed. She couldn't hide her surprise when Luciano the grabbed the white sheets and threw them on the carpeted floor. The laughter was gone and his expression mirrored that one of fury. Nina took a step back, wary of the next thing he would do.

"Did you know they would do this?" Luciano's focus was back on his wife. "Nina?"

The sheets? What do I tell him? What does he want to hear?

"My father told me about it. It's common practice in New Orleans to-"

"I'm aware of your practices." He gritted his teeth. "But it's the girl who is marrying into The Outfit. Not the other way around. We don't uphold the bloody sheet tradition. At least, not anymore."

As soon as the words left his mouth, Nina could feel her shoulders sag. She found great solace in his revelation. Now, she wouldn't have to experience the humiliation of her family seeing her virgin blood on a cloth that acted as a canvas.

Her relief faded when Luciano closed the space between them. Nina had to remind herself that even though the sheets wouldn't be used, he would still want to consummate their marriage.

Luciano held Nina by her arms. "Next time your family has plans of their own and you know about them, as my wife I expect you to tell me about them. Am I clear?"

She nodded and felt the need to explain herself. "I didn't think it would matter. I thought your family also abided by old traditions."

For a moment or two, Luciano searched her eyes before letting go of her. He faced his back toward her and crouched down to pick up the discarded sheets.

Nina frowned as her husband neatly folded it and headed toward the door. "What are you doing?"

"Making it clear to your family where I draw the line of their involvement in our marriage." Before leaving, he looked over his shoulder and said, "Go to bed. It will take a while."

Nina stood in the middle of the room, her wedding dress untouched. It took a second for her to process what had happened. She doubted whatever he would do or say to them would go over well.

Papà doesn't like people talking back to him. Luciano wouldn't do anything too rash, right? I should go and stop him. Nina moved toward the closed door but couldn't bring herself to lower the handle. What am I doing? I shouldn't go. I should do as I'm told and go to bed. She had no intention of experiencing her husband's wrath.

Nina stepped inside the bathroom and locked the door. She went to stand in front of the wide mirror and removed a countless amount of hairpins from her updo. When she locked eyes with herself, everything seemed to hit her at once. She would spend the rest of her life with Luciano. A man capable of partaking in horrendous crimes. The overwhelming feeling made her feel like bawling her eyes out. Quickly, Nina formed her hands into fists and focused on another emotion. She didn't want to cry. If she did, her husband would see her bloodshot eyes the next morning.

Stay strong.

Getting out of her dress wasn't without effort. Nina let the gown pool around her feet and stepped away from it. After taking a shower and washing her hair to get rid of the hairspray, she grabbed herself a towel and dried her hair.

I've been in here for a while but I still haven't heard Luciano come in. Nina shook her head and checked her reflection. This is better. I don't want him to see me in this nightgown. It doesn't cover anything! It might as well be lingerie. What was Mamma thinking by picking this one for me?

Nina stood by the door and listened carefully if Luciano was on the other side. It was silent. The room wasn't occupied by anyone else except for herself. In the off-chance, Luciano would enter the room that very second, Nina made a short sprint toward the bed. Hiding her body under the blankets and turning off the bedside lamps. The moment she laid down, she felt the exhaustion crash down on her. Playing the perfect bride from beginning to end had taken its toll.

I'm finally alone but this is the most anxious I've been all day.

Even though she wanted to fall asleep, Nina would stay awake until Luciano had returned.

He has been away for quite a while. Maybe I should go after all.

Before heading to Luciano, Nina draped herself in a long velvety bathrobe that hung in the bathroom. Exiting the room without it wouldn't be wise. The clothes she wore underneath the robe left little to the imagination.

He said he would go to my family. Surely, he didn't mean my whole family. Is he after Papà?

Nina picked up her pace as she walked the hallway with bare feet.

If I remember correctly, Papà's and Mamma's room should be around here. Room 219.

When she found the plate with the correct number engraved on it, her strides faltered. The door of her parents' room was slightly ajar. There was no doubt in her mind, she would find Luciano in there.

Instead of barging in the room, she peeked through the opening to try and see what she was walking into. The only thing she could make out were the crumpled up white sheets on the floor. She was at the right address. With caution, Nina pushed the door to let herself in. First thing she saw was the trembling figure she called her mother. It looked as if her mother had seen a ghost.

Evelyn's brown eyes darted to her daughter and quickly grabbed her arms. Her nails digging into Nina's skin.

"Don't just stand there, go and help your father!" her mother snapped and her voice hysterical.

It was only when Nina saw what Luciano was doing, her mother's cry for help made sense. Her husband had her father pressed up against the wall, his fingers curled around the back of her father's neck. Nina wasn't sure whether she had come too late or just came in the nick of time.

"You broke the agreement. I hope this isn't indicative of future promises you make," Luciano's tone was harsh as he spoke to Carlos. "I don't appreciate people going around my back where my wife and I are concerned."

Nina's legs moved on their own, she had to stop Luciano. Her father's face getting more and more red by the second and the expression Luciano wore didn't bode well.

"Please, stop it!" Nina had her hand on Luciano's chest. "Don't do this, Luciano."

The bruising grip on Carlos his neck was gone and took this chance to put some distance between himself and Luciano.

Now, Luciano's attention was on Nina. The narrowing of his eyes at her made her fear the worst. Foreboding thoughts of Luciano lashing his anger out on her began to form.

"Didn't I tell you to stay in the room?" Luciano said to her.

Nina didn't get the chance to speak as her father beat her to it.

"If I'm being honest, I could have you killed for this." Carlos' chest heaved up and down while Evelyn massaged the back of his neck.

"And if I am being honest, my patience with you is running thin." Luciano clenched his jaw.

Both men knew Carlos his threat was empty. The Outfit wouldn't stand for it if a Gallucci was killed. A war would break out. Something The Outfit and the New Orleans Family couldn't afford. Neither families were at the height of their powers which was why an alliance between the two had to be made.

For this wedding to end without any bloodshed was in their best interest.

"We should go, Luciano," Nina said, not wanting their fight to escalate any further.

"I'm not forgetting this when I become Don, Carlos. You and Don Galasso owe me a favour."

Carlos didn't say anything in return.

Luciano addressed everyone in the room and continued, "Nobody will speak of this."

Carlos nodded. "That's better for everyone."

Luciano bit back a snarky comment at his father-in-law and faced Nina. "If you want to greet your parents one last time then you should do it now. We are leaving for Chicago first thing in the morning."

"No, it's fine. Can we go now?" she said, matching the low volume he had spoken in.

Luciano was perceptive and realised Nina wanted to protect her parents from him by leaving as soon as possible. He wasn't going to question her reasons. It didn't matter to him. Luciano and Nina left without another word and returned to their own room.

Nina watched Luciano disappear into the bathroom and emerge not much later. With the tuxedo gone, his boxer was the only piece of clothing on his body. He might have been stripped of his clothes and was no longer armed but her husband was as unnerving as ever. Nina couldn't take her eyes off his lean body.

"Can I take your staring as an invitation?" he drawled.

She tried to make out his expression as a few rays of moonlight shone on him. The shadows still obscuring most of his face. Her lips were parted, ready to speak but nothing came out. Nina knew from the tone of his voice, he wasn't serious. Earlier, she had been perfectly capable of speaking her mind. Being alone with him in a shared bed made her feel a little too vulnerable. Nina opted for a sitting up rather than lying down, hoping to regain her control. The blanket had gathered on her lap and her back rested against the headboard.

"What did you do?" Nina said in her desirable calm tone. "What happened?"

Once Luciano found out from Carlos that Don Galasso orchestrated for the bloody sheet tradition to happen, he wanted to storm over to his side. However, Luciano knew he was in no position to act on his own. He couldn't create a dispute between the two families without consulting Don Nicolò. It was a hard pill to swallow but Luciano had to let go of the disrespect New Orleans showed on his own wedding day.

"What do you think? Your uncle is not a man of his word. On both sides, it was agreed that the sheet tradition wasn't going to happen but apparently your uncle didn't agree. That is what happened, Nina. In our world, a man's word holds a lot of weight. Men who break their promises to me are met with an unpleasant version of myself."

Luciano might have been beyond saving but even he had his qualms about certain things. The depraved tradition of New Orleans was one of them.

Her husband's last words confirmed she did right in separating him from her father.

So, Uncle Galasso planned on pushing his beloved tradition from the start and Papà knew about it? Maybe it's a good thing Papà didn't get me someone from New Orleans. I knew they placed a lot of importance on a woman's virtue but to this extent? I didn't know.

"What are you doing? Go to sleep. We have to get up early."

In the morning? I thought we wouldn't leave for Chicago until tomorrow afternoon.

Nina obeyed and laid down. She stared at the ceiling, waiting for Luciano to fall asleep first. When he did, Nina let the darkness consume her as well.

By the time she got out of it a new and unknown life awaited her.

9

CHAPTER 9

Chicago Setting foot in Chicago wasn't as climactic as Nina expected it to be. She was calm. Too calm. Her facial expression stayed passive as they drove the streets of Lincoln Park. The grand mansions didn't do anything to change it either. Given that she was born in the family of an underboss, she had lived all her life in luxury. It was nothing new to her.

It feels as if I'm still in New Orleans. Nina stole a glance at her husband. Except for him, of course.

They passed the tall iron gates and a small white-painted guardhouse. Nina let her eyes explore the mansion's exterior and the greenery outside. Two lines appeared between her brows. The insides of Luciano's home were silent, yet, there were made men guarding the grounds of their superior.

"How many men do you have guarding the house?" she asked Luciano.

"During the day there are three including Bartolomeo and the night shift consists out of five men."

Isn't that a little overkill? Even Papà didn't have that many.

Luciano killed the engine and they got out of the car.

"Bartolomeo?"

"You'll meet him later. Stay here. I need to get something."

Nina stood on the sandstone paving as she watched Luciano walk back to the guardhouse from earlier. While her husband spoke to the man inside it, Nina took in the details of the two-story mansion. It had a sandy colour. Rows of glass she couldn't see behind because of the curtains. Each window had a railing with an intricate design. She liked them; unlike the window guards caging her in New Orleans.

"Nina," Luciano's voice pulled her out of her daze.

He beckoned for her to come to his side. She walked the short distance, her focus on the folded paper Luciano tucked inside his suit jacket.

A report from the guards? It's probably from yesterday. Our wedding day. Surely, he wouldn't file away every report made by them. Had something out of the ordinary happened? Something I should worry about?

In spite of her concerns, Nina wouldn't give them a voice. Her father's warnings had been drilled into her mind. He had strongly discouraged Nina to stick her nose in business.

Instead of going straight into the mansion, Luciano made her go around it. A petite building came into sight, sturdy trees casting shadows over it as they neared the backyard.

"This is where the guards can take breaks," he said to Nina and swung the door open. "Bartolomeo."

Nina saw the man take his shoes off the table and stand up. He looked startled. She examined his features, making sure to remember his face. Fine lines near his eyes, non-existent brows, low cheekbones and dark hair. Nina guessed he was around his forties.

"He will be your guard from now on."

Nina smiled politely and shook the man's hand. "It is a pleasure meeting you, Bartolomeo."

Bartolomeo answered with a terse nod. "Is there something you need me to do, Boss?"

It took Nina a second to realise he was speaking to her. Nobody had ever called her Boss. In New Orleans, her guard addressed her on a last-name basis. The change would take her some getting used to. Nina glanced at Luciano before looking back at Bartolomeo.

"No, thank you." Her smile still in place.

"You can continue your break," Luciano said to him. "Come, Nina."

"We'll speak another time then," Nina said to her new guard before exiting the building.

Nina couldn't help but compare Bartolomeo to her previous bodyguard Orlando. While Orlando had been young and fit, Bartolomeo was on the older side and slim. Cogs and gears rotated in her head as to why her husband had chosen Bartolomeo to be her guard. In her past, the topic of choosing her guard was something she didn't have any say in. Nina would rather not question Luciano, but this concerned her own safety. She wouldn't stay quiet.

"Why him?"

Luciano came to a stop and arched his brow. "Is there a problem?"

"What did Bartolomeo do before you appointed him as my bodyguard?"

"And you think it would appease your mind if you knew? He used to be the main enforcer of The Outfit and would still be if it weren't for you." His gaze cut to Nina. "You don't know him yet so I don't blame you for not trusting him, but Bartolomeo will do as is expected of him. My men know their priorities. As my wife, you are the safest woman in Chicago."

"Wouldn't that be the Don's wife?" Nina voiced and immediately wanted to take it back. She hadn't seen Don Nicolò be accompanied by anyone yesterday.

"No." He brushed the soft locks of hair off her shoulder. "My grandmother is dead."

For the first time, Nina felt for him. Judging from the look in his eyes, she could figure out that he shared a close bond with his grandmother. She too used to have that with hers.

"I'm sorry for your loss."

Luciano didn't say anything in return, not sure whether his wife was being genuine or only spoke the words because it was appropriate.

They proceeded toward an extension of the house made of glass. Luciano opened the French doors leading into the sunroom.

Nina didn't get a chance to properly take in her surroundings as her husband was quick to move on. It didn't matter though. She knew herself well enough to know she would be a frequent visitor of the open room. Nothing beat getting kissed by the sun and viewing the outside landscapes.

The living room was in stark contrast with the sunroom. Dark wooden floors on which the ornate chandelier's light glowed. Polished furniture that complimented the other masculine touches sprinkled throughout the space. It was imposing like her husband. She thought it fitted his image.

Luciano checked the time on his watch, cursing when he realised how much time had passed. His wife's eyes were trained on him.

"You will have to see the rest of the house by yourself. The boxes you sent are upstairs in the dressing room, it's right next to our bedroom. I figured you wanted to unpack them yourself," he said to which she nodded in response. "I need to go now."

Instead of walking away, he stepped toward her. Her heart beating faster with each step he took. She stood her ground and accepted her husband's piercing gaze; one that would make most people wince. His light touch on her throat felt intimate. Too familiar.

"Are you going to let me in on your thoughts?"

Goosebumps hidden by her loose hair rose along the back of her neck.

"My thoughts? About?"

"Me," his voice lower than before.

"I think I'm incredibly lucky to have a husband as wonderful as yourself." Nina showed Luciano her signature smile and to put the cherry on top of it, she kissed him on the cheek.

Luciano smiled, his eyes not matching its warmth. His expression bore some semblance to discontent. His attempt to get his wife flustered failed once again. Wanting to get more of a reaction, he pressed his hand against the side of her neck. His thumb used to create tingles across her jaw. Nina's pulse hummed against the feel of his palm.

"That is quite the textbook answer you got there. I suppose it will be perfect for when you meet other Outfit members."

"And to not disappoint those very same men, you should go before you're late. Didn't you need to go somewhere?" Nina looked at him innocently.

Luciano removed his hand from her. The heat never truly leaving her skin.

"I should be back by midnight," he said before leaving through the front door of the mansion.

As if she was holding her breath, Nina let the air from her lungs escape. She slumped against the back of the leather couch using her arm to steady herself.

I could barely bring myself to speak to him last night and now I'm kissing him like the good wife I am.

Nina was well-aware of the reason behind the change in her behaviour. In the bedroom she felt as if she was at his mercy. Outside it, she had her usual confidence backing her up.

What did he even have to leave for? We just got here from the airport and he has to go again? At least I can have some time by myself now.

She pushed herself off the couch and strolled around. The kitchen was the first space she stumbled upon. It matched the sitting room. The light marble countertops were refreshing compared to the dark colour of the cabinets. Wondering what the view was like behind the roller shades, she used the cord and saw the gates and white guardhouse again. Luciano's car wasn't on the driveway anymore. Nina dropped the shades and moved on, opening and checking the inside of each door she passed in the hallway.

It's locked.

She let go of the door handle and tried the door next to it. Letting her legs do as they pleased, Nina checked out all the lined-up books in the library. She seated herself on the chaise lounge and picked up the open book that laid on the small table.

Saint Patrick's Day.

The book's title made her eyebrows raise, but not as much as hearing her name get called. It was Bartolomeo's voice. Quickly, she tossed the book aside and went back to the living room.

"Yes, Bartolomeo?"

He turned around to face her. "Teodoro is currently in front of the gates, Boss. Should I let him in or send him away?"

He is asking me? It had slipped her mind she was now the lady of the house. She wasn't used to people asking her what she wanted. Well, flat-out refusing him would be rude.

"You can let him in."

10

CHAPTER 10

Nina paused for a full minute in the foyer before welcoming her guest inside, suiting up for her role as the perfect well-mannered lady she was raised to be. Opening the front door revealed the tall figure that was her brother-in-law.

"Good morning, Teodoro. I wasn't expecting you." A gracious smile was painted on her features.

"I never tell Luciano ahead of time when I'm coming." He nonchalantly lifted his shoulder, creating creases in his dark-green dress shirt. "Good to see you again," Teodoro said and invited himself in.

I wish I could say the same.

Nina closed the door – a little harder than intended – and trailed after him into the main area. Feeling confused why he had come to visit her.

"And what brings you here, Teodoro?" she kept the tone of her voice neutral, not letting him know how unwanted his sudden appearance was.

He moved his head from side to side seemingly looking for someone. "How odd. Luciano is not here?"

Either he needs to polish his acting skills or he is playing around.

"He left not too long ago."

"Did he now?" Teodoro sat down on one of the armchairs, swung his arm behind it and displayed a bored look.

"You don't look all that surprised to me."

The corners of his lips quirked up. "Can't say I am. I didn't think you would call me out on it though. I'm sure we'll get along."

Nina chose not to comment on his remark. "Can I get you something to drink?"

Teodoro shook his head and motioned at the couch, suggesting she'd join him.

Nina obliged and crossed one leg over the other, her hands on top of each other on her lap. She regarded the young man sitting across her. He had a casual way of speaking, his actions matching accordingly. Despite his attempt to come off in a certain way, Nina couldn't rid herself of the unease at his presence.

"I see my brother upped the security. Not sure if it's because of everything that has been going on or because he has his lovely new wife to protect."

Everything that has been going on? As in Luciano becoming the future Don? I guess The Outfit is going through some changes right now. A new ally and soon enough a new leader. A new Don. My husband.

For the slightest moment, pity flashed across his face. "I must say that I didn't expect Luciano to be this eager to work again. Leaving you to fend for yourself on your first day here. I do apologise on my brother's behalf."

Nina could tell Teodoro wasn't sincere in his apology and it royally ticked her off.

"There is nothing for you to apologise for. I'm perfectly capable of taking care of myself," she said with a small smile. "It can't be helped if he has to work. I never asked but what do you do?"

"I am a soldier unlike Luciano who is a capo right now."

Soldier. So, the same as Giorgio.

"I'm sure Luciano will appreciate that. What you said about taking care of yourself." He laughed to himself before saying, "I can't imagine him keeping his sanity with a clingy wife at his side."

"What makes you say that?"

"Nothing really but I know Luciano well enough that he wouldn't want someone like that."

"Good to know."

Nina penned his comment down and put it in her imaginary drawer. She knew she didn't have to give it too much thought. Relying on others and being needy seldom happened.

Teodoro lifted his forearm from the armchair, his palm showing. "So, tell me about New Orleans. What is their Don like?"

There it is. He came here for intel.

"I wouldn't know. I only know him as my uncle." The only time Galasso had spoken to Nina as her Don was when he informed her of the wedding date.

"That's too bad. How about your father? He is their underboss, right?"

She considered her answer. "Strict. He expects complete obedience from his subordinates. Nobody is my equal – is something my father would say."

Subordinates. His pawns. Like me. Nina's gaze fell on the new piece of gold wrapped around her finger. It reminded her she was no longer in her hometown. No longer obliged to listen to her father.

Teodoro opened his mouth to ask another question but the buzzing against his leg stopped him from doing so. He moved toward the edge of his seat and grabbed the phone out of his pocket. The name displayed on it made him raise his eyebrow.

"Did you tell my brother I came here?" He lifted his gaze to meet Nina's.

Should I have?

"No."

Nina stayed silent as Teodoro accepted the call. His answers were short, not revealing the nature of his conversation with Luciano. Not even a minute had passed by and the call came to an end. He put his phone away and stood up.

"I'd love to keep you company but my brother seems to miss me."

Nina moved to stand up so she could walk him to the door.

Teodoro held his hand up. "I can walk myself out. I'll come by another time." The sound of the front door closing was Nina's cue she didn't have to hold up appearances any longer. She rounded her shoulders, brought her hands to her face and massaged sore cheeks from all the smiling she had done.

Nina dropped her arms to the side and stared at the wide black screen of the television. Turning it on showed her footage of several security cameras. All of them were shots from outside the mansion. She could see everything that was going on in the front, sides and the back of the mansion. There were even cameras pointing at the road near the iron gates. Nine of them in total. The lower-right footage caught her attention, the gates opened and a car drove off. Teodoro had left the grounds.

He is probably going to where Luciano is. Wherever that might be. Nina made the screen go black again and sighed. Still have the rest of the house to explore and I should get to unpacking my stuff.

Nina made her way to the foyer where she was greeted with a grand staircase. She climbed the curved stairs, reached the top and stood in the middle of a long hallway. Her heels barely made any noise against the runner rug as she checked out the rooms on the right side. Once she turned the corner at the end of the hall, she found the dressing room Luciano had told her about.

"Finally."

The room was sectioned in two parts. One side was filled with Luciano's wardrobe and the other side was empty, ready to be stuffed with Nina's clothes.

"Better get these off," she mumbled and put her heels to the side.

Not wasting any of her time, Nina got to work and unpacked the boxes. It took a while before she had finished the task of organising everything in the closet. Some clothes were in dire need of ironing. Especially, her evening dresses that she had been forced to fold due to the box its size. That task, however, she would leave for another day to be done.

Nina was delighted when she checked the time on her phone. Four hours in total. That's quicker than I expected.

She held her arms above her head to stretch and exhaled. Nina was done with her work but instead of heading toward the door, she moved to Luciano's side of the room. Her fingers lightly touching the sleeves of his dress shirts. She stopped at the sight of expensive watches displayed underneath a glass surface.

He's a collector. Who would have thought?

Nina opened the drawer, thinking she would find more watches but only saw knives. The same type of combat knives Nina used to see in her brother's room. She checked the second drawer.

More knives?

No. Guns.

"I've seen enough for today."

After closing the drawer and lowering herself on the ottoman bench in the middle of the room, Nina ran a hand through soft brown hair. Thinking of her brother made her want to hear his voice again. Before long, she waited for Giorgio to answer her call.

He picked up at the first ring.

"Nina! What took you so long? I thought that motherfucker confiscated your phone or something like that."

Nina was quick to think on the spot and lowered her voice by a few octaves. "Hello, Giorgio. This is motherfucker."

Both laughed immediately at Nina's poor imitation at Luciano's voice. Her eyes slightly tearing up. It had been a while since she allowed herself the luxury of laughter.

"But for real, how are you doing?"

The worry lacing his voice caused water droplets to pearl down her cheeks. Nina waited with answering, knowing the tremble in her voice would give the truth away.

"Nina?" Giorgio said when his sister stayed silent. "Can you not speak right now? Is Luciano there?"

She shook her head. "No, I'm alone. He left for work hours ago. I'm fine, Giorgio."

"Really? I thought you would be- Nevermind. If you are doing fine then that's all that matters."

Nina heard her brother mutter curse words and loud thuds of him going the stairs up. "Are you okay?"

"Yeah, Dad just came home. I'm in my room now."

"But he usually works from home." She frowned.

"I know but Uncle Galasso called him over for something."

The sheets. Did Papà tell Uncle Galasso what Luciano had done? There was never a presentation of the sheets, so he must know. I'm sure Papà told Uncle Galasso a different version of the truth. One that shines a better light on him. Regardless of Luciano's warning to stay quiet, Papà is still compelled to inform his Don of the incident. Nina hugged herself with her arm.

"After all of you returned home, did Papà mention anything about Luciano?"

"No. Why?"

That's good. I can leave it behind me.

"I was just wondering."

11

CHAPTER 11

When the clock struck twelve, lights from the hallway peeked into the darkened master bedroom. The heavy door shut and the ray of light was gone.

Nina was unmoving as she laid in bed. Slowly, she lifted her gaze to see Luciano walking toward the bathroom. The door was left open and light flooded into the bedroom again. Nina went to lie on her back as she listened to the stream of water hitting the tiles. She momentarily closed her eyes, opening them again when she heard a click.

"Good night," Luciano said as he got in his side of the bed.

She moved her head sideways, facing him. "Good night."

The faint scent of cigars Nina got teased with earlier had been replaced by a fresh and clean woodsy aroma.

"Can I ask you something?"

"I'm not stopping you."

Silver eyes were directed in her way resulting in the question she initially wanted to ask to die on her tongue.

"Do you smoke?"

"And you would like to know?"

"I smelled it on you."

"I've gotten myself quite the observant wife." Amusement danced in his eyes. "I don't smoke. My grandfather does."

Neither engaged in any further conversation. Nina stared back at the ceiling, thinking back on the guest she received earlier that day. Teodoro's throwaway comment about the security had been gnawing at her. She wanted to be in the know.

Her father's warning whispered through her mind. Questioning men would not be welcomed with open arms according to him. Lips parted and locked. One part of Nina was ready to bring her voice to the surface and the other ready to drown it.

Will he get angry with me? Will he ignore me? She exhaled softly at the possibility. I could try.

"Your brother came here." Nina slid her gaze back to him. "He mentioned something about you having more security."

"Yes, he told me all about it. It's true."

Is he willing to tell me more?

She tried her luck. "Is it because you are next in line? Is that why you were with your grandfather?"

"It's because of the Irish." A grim expression fell over his features, the darkness doing nothing to hide it. "You should know that they are more active over here than in New Orleans." Chicago was not in its entirety ruled by the Gallucci family. There were plenty of rivals who had laid claim on other parts of the city – MC clubs, Hispanic-American street gangs, Bratva and The Irish Mob. Most of them were not big enough to cause problems, much less bring a full-on war to The Outfit for more territory. Only one syndicate had the manpower to do so.

The North Side Irish Mob had been posing as a problem for decades. A constant force to be reckoned with. Four years ago, they had been the cause of alarm amongst The Outfit families. The Banion Family was a glaring red dot on Luciano's radar. Once Luciano was the Don, he planned on cutting their numbers in half by marching a war. An act of violence to put the scorching flames inside him to rest.

"Did something happen with The Irish?"

"One of Banion's guys was on stakeout yesterday. He was watching the house."

What if there is someone outside right now?

A chilling sensation ran along her spine. The mere idea of a lurking enemy watching their every move was unsettling.

"I need to get up early. Any last questions?"

"No, thank you."

"For?"

"Answering me."

Once again, a striking silver focused on Nina and this time longer than before. He watched her as if she was an enigma he might never be able to solve.

Waking up in a different bedroom took Nina some getting used to. Even though she was alone in the house, she still made sure to look sophisticated. Nina let her steps lead her to the kitchen for breakfast. She eased past the door and stilled when another person caught her attention. Composure returned quickly to her side seeing that it was only a maid. The woman's dark-grey hair showed her age but her radiant smile cut off a few years.

"I'm thrilled to finally meet you, Mrs Gallucci. I hope you got a good night sleep."

"I did. Thank you." A polite smile was given by her. "And what do I call you?"

"Oh, yes! Pardon my rudeness. It's Serena."

Nina picked up on the flustered manner she spoke in and assured her that it was fine. She moved over to the coffee machine and let a cup be filled with the hot beverage.

"I didn't see you yesterday," said Nina and glanced at the old maid.

"We only come twice a week. The middle and at the end of the week."

"Where is the other maid?"

Serena checked the time on the wall clock. "She's cleaning the hallways and rooms now. I should start preparing dinner. I'll make my specialty!" her voice became chirpy.

"I'm sure it will be delicious."

"You deserve only the best as the Don's wife." Her eyes widened at the slip-up in her words. "Oops! I mean Capo of course but with the official announcement coming up it almost feels as if he is already the Don."

She knows quite a lot but not in the same way the maid at home knew things. Serena doesn't strike me as someone who spends too much time gossiping.

I like her.

"That reminds me of something. Have you seen Bartolomeo around?"

"I think he might be taking a break but don't take my word for it. I'm not sure."

"Okay, I'll get out of your hair then." She emptied the cup, the hot liquid warming her up from the inside.

Nina left and went straight to the guards' quarters in the garden. It didn't look as if anyone was in the building from the outside.

Nevertheless she knocked on it but as was expected the action didn't elicit a response.

Maybe one of the guards at the front will know.

She was quick to make her way to the gates and spotted her bodyguard speaking to the man inside the small guardhouse. From the corner of her eyes, Nina noticed another made men on guarding duty. Bartolomeo looked to be the oldest and thus the most experienced out of the bunch.

"Good morning, Mrs Gallucci," the man inside the guardhouse said to which Nina replied accordingly.

"Good morning, Boss. Can I be of help?"

"Yes, there is one thing I'm curious about. I was wondering if you could help me with it?" Nina stepped away from the guardhouse to move the conversation elsewhere and Bartolomeo followed suit.

"Anything. I've been instructed to follow your orders before anyone else's."

Even Luciano's?

"I'm sure there is a list of all the underbosses and captains but where can I find it?"

His eyes slanted her a look. To Nina, it didn't appear as if he was expecting her to ask for such a thing.

"My best guess is that you will find it in Luciano's office."

That makes sense.

Wait. Did he just call him Luciano? Not Boss like he does with me or even Capo?

It was hard for Nina to hide her surprise since nobody in New Orleans ever addressed their superior on a first-name basis. Before Bartolomeo's dark eyes re-focused on her, she shoved the feeling away, masking her face along with it.

He held out a keychain for Nina to take and added, "You'll need this. Luciano always locks his office when the help comes over."

She thanked him and plucked the keys out of his palm.

"Is there anything else I can do, Boss?"

"No, that was all."

Her bodyguard nodded. "If you need me I'll be making rounds on the grounds."

The two parted ways and for the first time Nina entered her new home through the front entrance. She had a good guess which room was Luciano's office and tried unlocking the door next to the library. She hit the nail on the head.

Luciano's study was panelled with rich wood. Built-in shelves were on either side of the walls. There were no windows despite the space being located on the first floor. Dark shades of brown were seen throughout the space.

She walked past the sitting area in the middle and reached the other end of the room where a large desk and chair stood. Her eyes scanned the shelves. Finding the documents wasn't hard. Everything had been neatly organized. Nina lowered herself on the large chair, the papers in her hands and began memorizing its contents.

As the wife of the next Don, it was only natural she knew the names and faces of high ranking made men.

Some of the names sounded vaguely familiar. Many introductions had been made during the wedding though Nina couldn't remember half of them. The constant stream of people coming and going to congratulate the newlywed were too many names to remember all at once.

12

— ● —

CHAPTER 12

Indigo hugged Nina's body like second skin once she zipped the back. Hints of gold were sprinkled throughout her jewellery. The second drop earring was picked up the same time her husband entered the dressing room. Nina spun around while securing the earring in its place and watched him from afar.

In the past week, Nina had spent most of her days alone. Luciano was away a lot, constantly working and preparing for his new role in The Outfit. Instead, Teodoro had been keeping Nina company. Her brother-in-law kept true to his words and visited her another two times. So far, she knew him better than her own husband.

The minute Luciano entered the dressing room, he couldn't take his eyes off of her. She was alluring to him. Whenever they shared the same space, his gaze gravitated toward Nina.

While he was checking her out, Nina did the same to him. His hair was slicked back, not a single strand out of place. He wore a crisp white dress shirt, the collar standing up, black dress pants and polished shoes.

It was the day when Luciano would officially become the Don of The Chicago Outfit and a celebration would be held in honour of it.

"Are you ready?" he asked before heading to his side of the room and grabbed something. He went to stand in front of the long mirror against the wall, his hands tying a tie and grey eyes flickering over to Nina.

"Yes," she replied, smoothing out her evening dress.

"I didn't mean it in the literal sense. There will be a lot of new faces for you. Are you nervous?"

"No."

Once the collar was fixed and the suit jacket on him, Luciano bridged the short distance between them. "I hope you will be capable of giving a little bit more than one syllable responses when you meet the rest of the family." He caressed her cheek with a feather-like touch.

Nina's lips stretched up into a tight smile. "I know what I have to do."

"Will I get a preview?" He pushed for more.

Nina was torn on what to do. Adhere to his wish and give him what he wanted or give him the cold shoulder.

"You'll see it once we get there," she said and stepped away.

Luciano's arm shot out, caging her. "So you will be the loving wife I was promised?"

The change in the air made her feel an inch smaller. The patter of her heartbeat was no longer steady as she was backed up against the wall. Her face, however, didn't reveal anything. It carried the same calm it always did.

"Always," Nina replied, and by force of habit, her lips pulled into a sugar-sweet smile.

She watched his brows draw together, his eyes narrowing along with it. There was a stretched silence before he spoke again.

"We need to be early to welcome the guests." He dropped his arm. "Come."

They proceeded to leave for the celebratory event which was held at Nicolò's mansion. It was tradition that the official announcement be held and hosted by the previous Don. It was like that when Luciano's father became Don and it was the same now that it was his turn.

Driving to Luciano's grandfather seemed to be over in a flash, not strange considering he lived in the same neighbourhood as them. The gates already stood wide open and made men with rifles were posted on either side of the road. Luciano parked the car and they got out, his hand rested on Nina's lower back, guiding her to the Victorian style mansion. They passed another two armed men guarding the entrance and got greeted by Nicolò.

"It is good to see you again, Nina," said Nicolò and turned to Luciano. "Nero is already here. Why don't you go to him? He had something to discuss with you and it's still a while until people start coming in."

Nina could tell by the subtle change in Luciano's expression that he wasn't eager on leaving her side. She found it a little peculiar since that was the exact thing he had been doing for the past week. He glanced one last time at her before disappearing.

"How is Chicago doing it for you?" his voice was gruff.

"I'm having a good time so far. Thank you for your consideration."

Fine lines near Nicolò's mouth accompanied his faint smile. "Your father wasn't lying when he told me you were a true lady but there is no need to be so formal. Save that energy for when the guests arrive."

"I apologi-" She stopped herself and smiled apologetically. "It's hard to shake off."

"Tell me if I am mistaken but you look a little nervous."

"Do I?"

"Not really, no." He laughed softly. "But I'd be surprised if you weren't feeling it."

"I am." There was no point in denying the truth to, what was essentially, a human lie detector. "Only a little though so I'll manage."

"Good because they're here." Nicolò gestured she take a look at the open doorway where a middle-aged couple handed their coats to the catering staff.

"I'll get Luciano."

Nina found him in the main area. Her appearance had Luciano put his conversation with Nero to a halt. Now, both men their focus was on her. She addressed her husband and informed his presence was needed. By the time they returned to the foyer, Nicolò was speaking to the middle-aged couple.

"That's my Aunt Stella and her husband Raniero. He used to be the consigliere," Luciano made sure to lower the volume of his voice as they approached them.

A feeling of pleasant surprise washed over Nina when he informed her. She thought he would leave her to fend for herself which was why she had taken matters into her own hands.

"I know who they are but I appreciate the thought." She flashed him one of her sincere smiles.

Luciano kept his eyes on Nina as it was the first genuine smile he had ever gotten from her. Heavenly is how he'd describe it. He didn't want the rare sight to go away but knew it would once they joined the others.

For the better part of the conversation, Luciano's aunt did most of the talking.

"I can't wait to hear what you'll have to say, Luciano." Stella's smile deflated before adding, "We won't be able to stay for too long though."

"Yes, of course." Nicolò now looked at the dark-blonde haired man. "How are you feeling, Raniero?"

"I've had better days."

"I'll be sure to keep my speech short then," Luciano said.

After her husband's aunt and uncle moved on to the decorated main area, other guests began arriving in what seemed like an endless stream of people. The more time passed, the more her nerves faded away. By the time they were done welcoming all guests, Nicolò slinked out of the foyer to play host and the two of them stayed behind.

"I didn't expect you'd know the soldiers as well." A hint of appreciation flashed across Luciano's face.

"It's only natural besides I only know which family they belong to." Nina paused and said, "But I doubt they would care if I knew their given name. It's you whose attention they want."

"I strongly doubt you truly believe that." Luciano brushed over her wedding ring. "They care. Not only are you my wife but your connections to New Orleans are of importance."

"The elders don't seem to like that."

"Well, our families have been at war with each other in the past and, in a way, you represent them."

"So trying to win them over is a hopeless cause?"

"For the majority, yes."

As Nina listened to his murmured words, she followed his gaze, leading her to the ring. She looked up again, this time eyeing the women lingering by the entryway to the main area and received their curious looks thrown in her direction.

"We should go. People are starting to wonder where we are."

"No." He now had his other hand on her waist. "I'd to like stay here a little longer."

"Because?"

"I'm not all too fond of crowded places."

Noticing that her husband's tie was crooked, she moved her hand from his chest and carefully straightened it out.

"What are you doing?" he inquired, not being used to her gentle touch.

"Being the loving wife you want me to be." She met his gaze. "People are watching us."

He glanced over his shoulder and drawled, "You had me fooled. I suppose doing the same to them will be like breathing for you."

13

CHAPTER 13

The many families listened to their new Don speak as soon as he had addressed them. A sense of respect hung around. All hoped for Luciano's spoken promises to become true one day.

"This one's for you." Teodoro extended his arm so Nina would take the glass of champagne.

"No, thank you. I'm good."

"You can throw it away for all I care but you might want to raise a glass when he wraps his speech up."

Nina sighed softly, took the glass and re-directed her focus on her husband.

"We will take what they took from us. The Irish will lose this war and, as always, The Outfit will be victorious." Luciano held a crystal glass up in the air. "To family!"

"To family!" The Outfit repeated after their Don and copied his action, the clinking of glass was heard throughout the space.

Shortly after, Luciano returned to his wife's side, the champagne no longer in his hand. Together they looked perfect; both carrying themselves with confidence. It mattered not what city they were in, the evil eye would always be there to follow.

Teodoro opened his arms to give his brother a hug. "You did an amazing job just then. Then again what else to expect from a family man."

Luciano held up his hand, signalling that the affection wasn't welcome. "Don't try and distract me. What are you doing here? I told you to-"

"Work can rest for one night. Tonight is meant for celebration only. If I were you I'd thank me for keeping her good company." Teodoro looked expectantly at Nina for her to agree with him.

"And it's very much appreciated but if you have work to do, I won't hold you back," she said to him.

"Now that things are changing, I need you to grow up and be more serious, Teodoro." Luciano's tone rang cold and serious. "And as I have heard it, you've given Nina more than enough company in the past week."

"Oh? And who told you that?" His eyebrows shot up. "Bartolomeo or... was it you, Nina?"

"Stop feigning ignorance. You know the guards tell me everything," Luciano said, making his brother face him again.

"Don't tell me the same doesn't count for you wife." Teodoro searched for a hint of irritation on either Luciano's or Nina's face but ended up with nothing. "Are you sure you two are married? Or are you just not on speaking terms?"

If it was anyone else who had the audacity to ask such a question, Nina would have been taken aback but with Teodoro taken into the equation, she wasn't. At the same time, she didn't think he would actually say something like that out loud.

"You think you're so funny." Luciano laughed mirthlessly. "You are lucky you're my brother."

"That's debatable." Teodoro smirked, turned around and headed to his cousin.

Now that her husband's mood had taken a turn for the worse, Nina wished nobody else had taken notice of it. She could feel his eyes piercing through her skull as she drank the last bit of her sparkling champagne and put it on the tray of a passing waiter.

"Why didn't you tell me?"

"I did tell you your brother came to visit."

"Yes, one time. The others were left unaccounted for."

"Didn't you just say the guards already told you?"

"Yes, but you are the one that's supposed to tell me. I'm fairly certain I let you know what I expect of you."

"I just thought Teodoro told you about his visits like the first time." Bitterness fought with the outward smile on Nina. "When would I have told you anyway? You're rarely ever at home and when I do get to see you it's either very briefly in the morning or late at night."

What am I doing? I must be going mental for fighting him like this.

"You could have easily mentioned it at night. I know you stay awake until I get home. Why you even do that I don't know. You almost never say anything," he muttered the last part.

"Can we stop bickering? And I don't see how your brother coming over matters in any way," said Nina whilst feeling she was throwing gasoline on a fire.

"It doesn't. What matters is that we..." Luciano's voice trailed off as he saw his cousin approaching them. "We're not done yet."

The man in front of them was undeniably a Gallucci. With a large frame, midnight-black hair and an unnerving look in the eyes, Severino ticked all the boxes. The women next to him was roughly the same height as Nina and smiled in such a way that even children could tell it was fake.

"I need a quick word with you, Luciano." Severino didn't adjust the angle of his head and merely lowered his aloof gaze to meet Nina's. "If the lady doesn't mind."

"I don't mind."

The number of exchanges between Nina and Severino had been scarce but based on their first meeting and her observations on him, Severino appeared arrogant. Whenever she saw him speaking to anyone, he would quite literally look down on them as the conversation flowed; his impressive height making it all the more easy. In a way, Nina thought of Luciano and Severino as opposites. Throughout the evening, she had seen her husband treat others with respect – high and low ranked members alike – but Severino showed as if he only held contempt for others.

"I'm going to get a drink. Do you want anything, Nina?"

"That champagne was pretty nice," she replied to which Luciano nodded.

"What about you, Marietta?" Severino asked his wife.

Marietta flinched away from Severino's touch and shook her head to answer his question.

Not even a minute ago, Nina believed the air between her and Luciano was tense. It paled in comparison to the tangible strain she just witnessed in Severino's and Marietta's relationship.

Luciano cleared his throat, effectively making Severino rip his eyes off Marietta. "Come on."

When the men were out of earshot Nina asked, "Are you alright?"

A melodic laugh slipped out of Marietta's mouth. Definitely not the reaction Nina was expecting but a pleasant one nonetheless.

Seeing Marietta draw back from Severino's touch made Nina jump to the conclusion of domestic violence. Perhaps she had imagined the heavy air from earlier.

"Why wouldn't I be?"

Nina took note of the defensiveness in Marietta's tone and assured her that her question was only meant to make conversation. She gave her a gentle smile and received a distrustful look in return.

She's awfully guarded. The thought almost got Nina to scoff at herself. Who am I to judge? I'm basically the same as her.

"So, how long have you two been married?"

"Not that long." Marietta sighed, sadness radiating off of her. "About a year now."

"It can get better." She lightly touched Marietta's elbow.

Marietta shifted her weight and was now out of Nina's reach. "You don't know me and you should worry about your own marriage instead of mine."

Fair enough.

She continued, "I'm not trying to be disrespectful. Trust me, I'm not but for your own sake-"

"They're coming back," Nina warned as she saw Luciano and Severino returning to them.

Nina's thoughts were on Marietta's advice as she thanked Luciano for her drink. She looked over at the married couple; Severino and Marietta acted as if they hated each other's gut. The only question roaming Nina's mind was whether she and Luciano would also be like that in a year's time.

I'm being ridiculous. I will never let it get to that point. I can make my marriage work.

Luciano placed his arm around Nina's waist, applying pressure to make her pay attention. "Sure, we can come over for dinner sometime. What do you think, Nina?"

"Yes, that sounds lovely."

"Great then it's settled!" Marietta smiled widely.

Nina handed her full champagne glass to Luciano. "Could you hold onto it for a second? I need to go to the bathroom."

Instead of going where she said she would go, Nina sought shelter in the hallway. Panic had been creeping up her body. Years' worth of bottled-up emotions were threatening to reveal themselves.

I can make this work.

Long and deep breaths were taken by her and with her hands on top of her chest, she tried to stay calm.

I'll be fine.

Nina felt her eyes watering up and instantly tilted her head up, preventing any tears from falling out. The natural reaction of her body had Nina cursing.

Don't you dare cry. You can do this. Just stay strong.

She leaned against the wall, her vision darkened as she moved her hands to cover her face. When someone grabbed her right wrist, Nina's breath hitched in shock. She lifted her gaze, locking it with a scowling Luciano.

"What happened?" He took hold of her other wrist to uncover all of his wife's face.

"What do you mean?"

"You look like you're about to cry, Nina."

"Why are you here?"

"You were gone for a while." Luciano moved closer, bridging what little space was left between them. "You're not telling what has gotten you like this."

"Nothing got me like this."

A tinge of annoyance flashed across his features. "Stop dragging this out, Nina. What is it? Did Non- my grandfather say something to you?"

"What? No." Her brows furrowing.

"Was it Teodoro?"

"No."

"Marietta?"

"No and can you please stop."

His grip loosened despite the burning in his grey eyes, frustration clear in them. Nina knew her husband wasn't a patient man to begin with and her silence didn't make it any easier. Luciano released his hold on his wife, turned his broad back to her and sighed heavily.

"You need to start talking to me."

She parted her lips but no words came out, unsure of how to convey her worries to him. Telling others what went around in her head was hard for her. Where her emotions were concerned, Nina was used to relying on herself – rarely on others and especially not strangers.

"I'm just a little homesick, that's all."

Luciano found it hard to believe she actually missed her family but made no comment on it.

"Are you coming with me or are you staying here?"

"I'll be there in a little bit," she said, watching him leave and began plastering a smile back in place.

14

CHAPTER 14

Another week flew by with Nina and Luciano not having made any improvements in their relationship. The result of this was only to be expected as neither saw much of the other. Nina needed to spend more time with Luciano if she was ever going to open up to him; practically impossible given the current state of affairs. To Nina, it felt as if she lived alone in the mansion since her husband was drowned with work.

Soft laughter came out of Nina as she read a text message from her cousin Rosaria. It was about yet another failed attempt at cooking. After poking fun at Rosaria and giving words of encouragement, she checked the time before turning her phone off.

Nina gazed up at the twinkling night sky. Just like she predicted, the sunroom quickly became her favourite place in the house.

"So this is where you are," Luciano mused as he entered the room.

"Were you looking for me?"

"Yes. Not for very long since I heard someone laughing."

Feeling exposed, she blushed. Her laugh from earlier contained more than a few snorts.

"Was there something you needed to tell me?" She immediately steered the conversation in the other direction, hoping he would forget her laugh.

"Severino invited us for dinner tomorrow."

That sounds thrilling. I'd rather spend a whole day with Teodoro than an evening with Severino.

"Okay."

Luciano grabbed the door handle, ready to close it and leave again.

He's going already? Nothing is going to happen between us if I allow it to. I can't hope for anything good to happen like that.

"Can't you stay?"

Both of them searched each other's eyes. She wondered what his next move would be and he tried guessing what she was thinking. Never before had his wife made a request like this and it made him wonder if she had ulterior motives.

"Is there anything you want?" He planted himself in front of his wife, his figure towering over her.

"Your company." It almost came out as a whisper.

His lips twitched as if she said something funny. Luciano lowered himself beside her, undoing the first three buttons of his dress shirt.

"I'll be honest, I thought you were going to ask for something else. I don't know why I forgot you aren't materialistic." He checked the ring decorating her finger. "You're not wearing the engagement one anymore."

Nina tensed by a fraction at the mention of the large diamond ring. "Do you want me to wear it?"

"That is up to you." That tiny smirk of his fell into a flat line. "Why do you want me here?" He laid his arm onto the sofa's back pillow, his fingers almost grazing her dark-brown hair.

Nina didn't break eye contact as his features set into a neutral expression. Honesty was the solution if she wanted them to be on the same page.

"You were right that night...I shouldn't keep you at arm's length."

"You do that with everyone from what I've seen," he said based on his assumptions.

"Not everyone. For example, I'm not like that with my family." After getting an eyebrow raised at her, she added, "Only some of them...or almost all of them but not everyone."

"Right, your brother being one of them I assume."

Nina nodded, a ghost of a smile appearing as she thought of Giorgio. "You don't like him, do you?"

"No, and the same goes for your parents."

I guessed that much but he really doesn't hold back, does he? Nina bit her lower lip, suppressing a smile.

"What is it?" he inquired.

"No, it's just what you said but thank you for your honesty."

"That's all you have to say?" The low rumble of his laugh had Nina's heart beating faster. "I openly admit I can't stand them and you thank me for my honesty? Are you sure you're Italian?"

Nina allowed herself to laugh along with him. When it became quiet again, she admitted, "I have no disillusions about what my parents are like, Luciano."

"You are more beautiful when you're like this. Your smile." He took her silky hair in his palm and let it slip through the gaps between his fingers. "When you're sincere."

Nina was no stranger to compliments from men but seldom did they do anything for her. She always reminded herself that those men did it to be in the favour of her father, the underboss. Now, it was different. Luciano had nothing to gain by speaking kind words and therefore, Nina knew he was being truthful.

Her blush deepened as they looked at each other. It was as if his fixed stare caressed her cheeks. She wanted to avert her eyes from Luciano but much like the first time she saw him but she couldn't bring herself to.

"How did you get it? You didn't have it when I met you?" She tapped her left temple, the same place where Luciano had a scar.

"The Irish were- are still after us. It happened a couple of months ago."

In an instant, a fierce quality in him came forward. Luciano was still the same daunting man from two years ago. Nina regarded her husband, wondering whether she had stepped on a land mine.

"You're not in danger if that's what you're thinking about. Since then, I've made the necessary changes," he said.

"I wasn't thinking about that."

Last time he brought The Irish up, a similar emotion showed in him. It's not just rage; there's grief as well.

The scar on his face wasn't anything distracting. It was small, the line was relatively straight and it had healed nicely. Carefully, Nina scooted over, only an inch left between them and gently traced along his scar.

"From a knife."

"Are they going to try again?" Nina stopped shying away from asking about the family business anymore. Her husband proved to be very open on the topic.

"I thought you weren't thinking about that?"

"Yes but now I am." She shifted her touch from his scar to his chest, feeling the rhythm of his heartbeat. It was on the faster side.

"They are planning to but that's all I can say. For now, we are pushing The Irish back so they won't be able to move around easily."

Whenever Nina expressed her concerns about a potential attack from The Irish, Luciano eased her by reassuring her safety; a side of him she appreciated.

"Are you sure you want to be this close to me?" The sensation of him placing his hand against the back of her neck made Nina sent him a questioning gaze. His thumb doing slow strokes along her hairline.

"What do you mean?"

Luciano made no mention of how his wife wouldn't come any-where near him in bed. Instead, he kissed her goodnight on the cheek and began leaving for their bedroom.

"I'm also going." Nina rose from the sofa and followed suit.

She went straight into the bathroom, locking it from the inside. Only when she finished showering, she could hear Luciano talking.

Who on earth would call him this late? It's almost midnight.

Nina threw nightwear on her body, brushed her hair and stepped into the bedroom again.

"There is no reason for me to lie about that. She simply can-not speak right now," Luciano said into the telephone and turned, hearing Nina's footsteps. "And you think I would waste my free time talking to you?" He handed Nina the telephone, saying that the call was meant for her before heading into the bathroom.

She brought the phone to her ear. "Hello?"

"I would have died if I had to listen to that guy for a second longer."

"Giorgio!" Her lips stretched up into a bright smile and the line between her eyebrows vanished. "How are you doing? Wait, why are you calling this late?"

"First of all, turn on your cell phone. I don't want another run-in with Luciano. Second of all, I don't get that much time off anymore. Things have been rough lately."

"Rough?"

"I can't say over the phone but we'll be fine. How are you holding up? That bastard better not have tried anything."

"God, Giorgio. Could you stop thinking like that? And no, he didn't." She sat down on the edge of the bed. "It's starting to get better actually."

"Really?" Giorgio sounded unconvinced. "You better not just say that to make me feel better."

"I wouldn't dare."

"I can hear you're smiling."

The clicking of the door got Nina to glance at Luciano coming out. He locked eyes with her, his hair was still damp as he ran his hand through it. She couldn't deny how good he looked.

"You still there, Nina?" Giorgio said when his sister fell quiet.

"What? No, yes, I'm here. Did anything else happen? How is everyone doing?"

"Nah and they are as good as can be but I'm gonna hang up now." He yawned loudly. "Kind of tired."

"Sweet dreams and take care of yourself, Giorgio."

"You too."

She returned the phone to its original place and got under the covers with Luciano.

15

—— ◆ ——

CHAPTER 15

Bright orange from the traffic light glared in Nina's peripheral vision as she stole a glance at Luciano. It was the same action he had been doing a lot that day. The light switched to green and they continued driving back to their home.

Dinner with Severino and his wife was strenuous – no one showed it though. Luciano and Nina were spectators to the married couple throwing passive-aggressive comments at each other. Eventually, Nina took on the job of diffusing some of the tension and succeeded.

One thing Nina couldn't ignore during their visit was how Luciano's attention stayed on her at all times and while it didn't interfere with her inherent sophisticated front, it did do something on the inside.

Once they arrived at the mansion, Nina climbed the curved stairs while Luciano stayed behind to have a word with a guard. She went to stand by the vanity mirror, took the bobby pins out of her updo and one by one, luscious locks fell down her back. Thanks to the mirror, she caught Luciano walking up to her from behind. She mentally prepared herself, her inner-voice repeating that she stay calm.

"Thank you for what you did at my cousin's place."

Her lashes fluttered as she looked downward. "It's the proper thing to do." She collected the pins in her palm and stowed them away.

"I know plenty of people that would have let the show continue on."

Nina raised a brow. "Like you did?"

"Something else occupied my mind."

"Yes, I noticed."

Luciano wanted nothing more than to break the icy facade she had mastered. He grabbed her by the arm and made her face him. "And yet you don't act like it."

Suddenly, it felt as if there wasn't enough oxygen for her to breathe.

His presence weighing heavy on her.

Their noses brushed against each other, her gaze flickered up to his eyes. They were half hooded, his desire for her almost feeling tangible. She let her own drop and noticed the ticking of his jaw. Then, her focus shifted to his lips. Nina wasn't sure what the cause of her next action was – be it his close proximity or the fact that he looked impeccable – but she closed the gap and gave him a kiss.

It was brief but the touch left a shimmering heat in its wake.

Nina began retreating but Luciano wasn't having any of it and so he stopped her from leaving what she started. "You shouldn't have done that." He cupped her face and let their lips collide once more.

Nina reciprocated, a daze falling over her. There was no denying how the feeling of him against her ignited a fire inside her. After a bit, she broke the kiss, needing to take a breath.

"Drawing the line?"

She brought her hands up to his and gently made him lower them. "I'm going to shower."

"Is that an invite?"

Judging by the tone in his voice, Nina could tell he wasn't serious but still told him that it wasn't.

Nina spread the newspaper out on the countertop, only reading articles that piqued her interest. She turned the page, the image of a running brown horse with its jockey on the far left corner and recognized him. Lancelot, the horse, had won the last couple of races as well. Nina breathed a sigh knowing the animal would be drugged. The last section of the write-up was left unread when Luciano appeared in front of her.

He didn't leave for work yet?

Her assumption was only natural since he wasn't next to her under the covers – the usual. From her peripheral vision, she noticed him gravitating toward her but kept her gaze on the papers. Not reading a single word yet acting like she did.

"That one is running today." He tapped twice on Lancelot's picture.

"And? Is he going to get one more win or will he lose?"

"If you're curious about it, you might as well go to see it for yourself." He folded the newspaper and looked at his watch. "The race begins in an hour."

Luciano waited expectantly on Nina as he held the door open. Going to a horse race was the last thing she thought she'd be doing today. Nonetheless, she followed his lead. To the racetrack it was.

Luciano and Nina arrived at the racecourse not long afterwards. The panoramic terrace gave them a perfect view of the course. The sun hid between the clouds. The track surface was covered in turf, the green colour fading in some places because of the many races that had taken place. An eager crowd waited right at the side lines, ready for it to begin although the starting stalls had yet to be filled with their horses and jockeys.

"It looks like we're early. We could go to the restaurant. Aren't you hungry?"

A little.

"No, I'm good. Thank you." She flashed him a small smile before reconsidering her answer. "Unless you are?"

He shook his head. "I'm not."

Thank God. I don't want to bump into any of those soldiers from earlier. I'm sure they also know who's going to win this race and made their bet. Nina spotted the same men sitting leisurely on the grandstand. Their pockets soon stuffed with dough. Does Luciano know they're here? Was he supposed to meet with them?

"Look, some of your men are here." She pointed them out.

He looked over at the soldiers. "I know."

"You're not supposed to meet with them?"

Luciano's brows drew together as he returned his gaze to his wife. His lips twitched as if it was the strangest question she could ask him. "No." At times like these, he really did wonder what thoughts swirled around in her head.

"Then why did you bring me here?" she asked carefully with a tinge of curiosity shining through her voice.

Immediately understanding settled on his expression. "You're my wife, Nina. Spending time with each other might do us some good. Did you expect me to only approach you when we make public appearances? Or is that what you were hoping for?"

"Don't put words in my mouth." She moved her head to the left, hidden away from his scrutiny. "I never said I didn't want to spend time together."

"Then say you do."

Long dark lashes shuttered her dismay from him. She quickly regained her calm exterior and faced him. The singe of his gaze felt too invading; despite them physically not being near each other, their shoulders not even touching, it felt as if his large hand sank in the delicate skin of her neck. His lips close enough to graze hers. His scent engulfing all of her.

"I do," her voice soft. Regret clawed at Nina. Admitting this simple thing already felt like she was baring her heart to him.

Luciano stayed silent for a minute. He expected her to give him one of her clever responses. Not the truth. In that moment, he got a glimpse of Nina's vulnerability.

A visible deep breath was taken and then she said, "It's beginning."

Luciano dragged his fixed look off of his wife and saw the horses appearing. Thirteen in total and their jockeys all in different colours.

"Who would you bet on?" he asked.

Nina checked out every horse with the exception of Lancelot and two other top contenders she had read about. "The black one in stall seven or maybe the one in four. What are their names?"

"Number seven is Galahad but I don't remember what the other horse is called."

Oh. He knows its name.

"My bet is on Galahad."

The loud trumpet played the tune of First Call, announcing the beginning of the race. The gates opened, freeing up the pathway for the horses to run. The turf track made for a slow start but the horses picked up their incredible speed. Had this match not been fixed and had Lancelot not been drugged, he would have the highest probability chance of winning. Alas, three black horses were out in the front – Galahad being amongst them.

"-and Galahad storms past them and takes the victory!" the announcer commentated with excitement.

"You won," Luciano said. "How did you know?"

"Lucky guess and a little bit of detective work. Oh, and your eyes stayed longer on that one compared to the others." She caught something flicker in his eyes though it disappeared too quickly to decipher. "Do you enjoy watching races?"

"You mean to ask if I enjoy watching them while knowing how the animals are treated," he said, hitting the nail on the head. "I couldn't care less. It's a good source for money making. I might feel bad if it were dogs instead. Don't tell me you actually care. You don't have to pretend to be a saint around me, Nina."

"It's called empathy." She felt like rolling her eyes at him. "You don't do dog races then?"

"No, that would be inhumane." He chuckled darkly. "Quite a lot of men used to do greyhound races but not so much anymore."

You have a twisted sense of humour, Luciano.

He continued speaking, "If you want to point a finger, you can direct it at the horse trainers. They are the ones accepting our offers."

"That's because the trainers don't know what they're getting themselves into."

Luciano nodded in agreement. "Most of them don't. When they do, it's only because they think they know."

It almost sounds as if he takes pride in his manipulation skills. Then again, it is a necessity in our life.

16

CHAPTER 16

"Their men have been keeping track of several families for some time now. They must already know of our arrangement with New Orleans considering a rather large group of us left the city to attend the wedding," Nero said as he presented Luciano with four printed photos of Irish soldiers and lined them up on the desk. "This one regularly drives by Nonno." He pushed the photo in Luciano's direction. It showed a man with a thin moustache and a goatee. "And- well, you already know but this one follows you," Nero said as he pointed at the picture on the far right.

Luciano grabbed the picture closest to him then muttered, "Even Nonno they won't leave alone." He folded it and tucked it in his back pocket. "Leave the other watchdogs be. I'll handle this one personally."

"If we attack, they will retaliate. Our men's lives are at stake." Nero implored his Don to change his mind.

Luciano flung him a hard glare. "They are on our territory."

"Yes, but they're not doing any funny business on our grounds," Nero said calmly. "Except for keeping an eye on us, of course."

"Stop playing devil's advocate."

"It's my job."

"Fine, you're fired."

The two of them let their eyes meet. The smirk on both their faces grew and soon evolved into chuckling.

"I'm happy to join if you plan on skinning him alive."

I'm sure you would, you sick fuck. Luciano knew exactly how depraved he himself could be sometimes. But his consigliere was far worse. Their pristine wear was truly nothing more than a flimsy cover-up for what laid underneath.

Luciano shook his head before Nero got the chance to let his imagination run wild. "I intend to send the bastard back to them. Alive, but handicapped." He stacked the other pictures on top of each other and stored them into the desk's drawer. "Maybe then they'll know not to walk into our streets without looking over their shoulder."

Keeping the Irish soldier alive was not showing mercy. Luciano's decision was nothing short of cruel. Surviving the dangers in that life without any handicaps was difficult as is. The man would be treated as nothing more than dead weight, and sooner rather than later his own comrades would put lead in his head for it.

"As your advisor, I have no complaints about keeping him alive. It's less likely to get picked up by the cops and feds but what about the promises you made during your speech. The family won't keep quiet if you don't deliver; lip service alone won't do."

"We'll have a proper war – in time," Luciano said, a thirst for it showing through his expression.

Nero remained silent, simply accepting the promise.

As Luciano and his cousin exited the mansion through the front door, he asked, "What time do you need to be at the hospital?"

Nero got in his car and read the time on his watch. "In an hour and thirty-eight minutes."

Luciano signed the gatekeeper to open the tall gates. "Say hello to your father for me," Luciano said to Nero, slammed the car door shut and watched him drive off.

He would've gone back inside the mansion if it wasn't for the glimpse he got of his wife. His steps lead him to round the corner, reaching the side of the house, and had to do a double-take when he saw Nina. A plaid button-up shirt, gardening trousers and bulky boots were not the things he was used to seeing on his wife. It fascinated him. With her back to him, she let her weight partly be supported by the shovel. His eyes swept the area. On his left were heaps of soil on the short grass and a row of holes in the ground. On his right were gardenia bushes waiting to be planted along the side of the mansion.

"You have to dig deeper if you want to fit a body in there," Luciano spoke up, making Nina turn on her heel.

She looked surprised. A sight he normally didn't get to see. He thought to himself that she appeared so much more at ease when she wasn't on her guard.

Nina emitted a sound similar to laughter and said, "Why don't you tell that joke to the guards? I'm sure you'll get a laugh out of them as well."

That was uncalled for.

"Don't like dark humour?" he inquired.

By now, Nina's spine was ramrod straight and her head held high. Back was the wary glimmer in her eyes. Her attempt to be more open to him proved to be more difficult than imagined.

"I do, but it's the fact that you've probably, if not definitely, done the thing you joked about."

I can hardly deny that.

"Why didn't you ask Bartolomeo for help? It would've sped things up."

It was true. The sky would still be a warm blue instead of sunset orange. Despite that, Nina didn't want anyone to help. She enjoyed gardening as it was something personal to her. Nostalgic.

"It's fine like this," she simply said and set the used shovel aside.

He watched as she lifted one of the evergreen shrubs, carried it and placed it into the large hole. She adjusted the position ever so slightly, grabbed the trowel and began putting soil in the places that needed it.

Without thinking too much about it, Luciano unclasped the expensive watch from his wrist and put it in the pocket. Then he did the same to his cufflinks and lastly, he rolled up the sleeves of his white dress shirt.

Nina glanced at him on her way to the second bush. "If you get any closer, your clothes might get dirty." She showed her smudged palms.

"Wouldn't be the first time." He lifted the shrub before she could and placed it next to the planted one.

"You don't have to help."

"Let me."

The soft timbre of his voice caught her in a daze. Intense, yet calming. Nina stopped herself from overanalyzing the situation and accepted his helping hand. She noticed how focused he was doing it. As if he didn't want to mess up.

While Luciano took the trowel from her, Nina retrieved another gardenia shrub and planted it. They continued to work like a well-oiled machine; their roles switching from time to time.

"They're the same as the ones at Carlos' house," Luciano commented as he reached out to touch the white petals.

"You remember?" Her gaze glided from Luciano to a single gardenia. She contemplated before sharing a part of her and finally told him, "They remind me of my Nonna. They always looked so pretty in her hair – big white flower against her black hair."

Luciano halted his actions and was all ears. He listened to her airy laugh, liking the melodic sound of it. Her laugh dwindled into a tiny smile, it painted a captivating image along with the sparkle in her brown eyes.

She continued speaking, "For the longest time I thought the colour of her hair was natural in spite of her age. It wasn't until later that I realised she dyed it."

The side of his lips curved upward. "It's a good thing you brightened up."

"Hey!" Nina smiled as she shot him a glare and nudged him in the side, getting dirt on his shirt in the process. She stilled for a second. Once again reminding herself who he was. "I'm sorry."

Luciano found it jarring how quickly her playfulness dissipated in thin air. He took note of her tense shoulders. His lips fell into a thin line. He gripped her wrist, a prominent scowl forming on his brows. "What are you apologizing for?"

"I got dirt on your shirt." Her cheeks heated and her eyes were glued on his shirt.

"So what? It will be clean once I wash it." He clipped. "You were relaxed before. Are you afraid I'll lash out on you?"

"Yes," she forced her answer out.

"I won't," he raised the volume of his voice by a fraction. Luciano roughly pressed his dirty palms against her rosy cheeks, brought them closer and said, "You're my wife, Nina."

She wasn't sure where the space between them had gone to but didn't mind it. Her breasts against his chest. Her breathing mingling with his. It wasn't even clear whose thundering heartbeat she was feeling.

"Do you understand? Or do I need to spell it out some more?"

She wanted to shake her head but his hands kept her in one place. Her hands held onto his veiny forearms, reminding him to let go but he didn't. "I understand," she said, her voice akin to a whisper.

His gaze drifted to her supple lips. They were close to his but not nearly as much as he wanted it to be. Luciano felt unhinged with want for her – had been for a while now. She was like a piece of art; seen by all and touched by no one.

Anticipation buzzed beneath the surface as she received the full weight of his stare. Deep and piercing. It made her fall under a spell.

"Luciano?"

The way his name rolled of her tongue was enough to let him know she wanted the same as him. The parting of her lips, the colour creeping onto her throat, the fluttering of her lashes. Their lips locked. He consumed her, taking all he could. There was nothing gentle about it. Their kissing was hurried and aggressive, both of them experiencing it as a drug.

She angled her head a bit more, giving him better access. A moan slipped out of Nina, her grip on his arms tightening. His warm tongue swept across her upper lip, creating electrifying tingles.

"The guards," her words were drowned as he kissed her again. She shifted her slim fingers from his arms to his hands, trying to get his attention. "They could see us."

"What?" his gravelly voice sent pleasant shivers through her spine.

"The guards are close by."

"I don't care." His lips grazed hers, tempting him to taste them again.

"It's a shame that I do care." She smiled sweetly. "And we're not done with the gardenias."

"Of course." Luciano dropped his hands and stepped back. Five more shrubs had to be planted. He returned his eyes to Nina, it was impossible to miss the dirt streaks on her face. "I'd say we're even now." Luciano tried brushing some of it away.

Nina recognized it was his way of trying to make her feel better. The pink on her cheeks bloomed and her smile morphed into a genuine one.

By the time they finished planting, a row of gardenia shrubs decorated the side of the mansion. Lush green bringing life into the picture.

A light sheen of sweat glistened on Luciano's forehead. The usually polished shoes were matted. Soil marked his clothes, especially the fabric at his kneecaps, and strands of dark hair were unkempt. Regardless, his looks still arrested Nina.

"Thank you for helping." She gave him a kind smile.

"It's fine." Luciano righted his hair.

Nina stifled a laugh, realizing he must have forgotten about the dirt on his hands.

The rising of his eyebrow at his wife was quickly followed by a string of curses when he looked down at his hands.

17

CHAPTER 17

The chain of the nightstand lamp got pulled on by Luciano, the room getting immersed in darkness. Faint in and exhales sounded nearby as Nina was in a dreamless sleep. The mattress dipped under Luciano's weight, his head on the end of the pillow and positioned in such a way that made looking at his wife easier.

No longer did she wait to fall asleep until he did. A small step in the right direction.

His gaze trailed over Nina's features, her lips getting more attention as he thought back on the dimples accompanying them when she smiled. Fondness beamed off of her when she had talked about her grandmother.

Maybe she did have good memories growing up.

Had she told him the truth about being homesick a few weeks ago? At first, Luciano didn't think twice about the notion. There was no way his wife missed her old life – considering how some family members treated her. Had his assumptions been wrong?

The sudden ringing of Luciano's cell phone ripped him out of his train of thought – and was loud enough to stir Nina out of her sleep.

Luciano grabbed his phone. Nero was calling. First thing Luciano asked was if something bad had happened.

"How do you say it? My old man got a heart attack. I'm at the hospital right now. There's no need for alarm. He's already up and kicking but I still had to let you know."

Luciano's eyes narrowed in scepticism. "Even though he's hospitalized?"

"Yes."

"When did he get it?"

"After returning home from a check-up at the hospital." Nero sighed heavily. "Talk about good timing."

"We're coming," he said and ended the call.

Nina was sitting upright against the headboard. Judging by Luciano's words, she guessed they spoke of a close relative and not one of the made men. There should have been no reason for her to come along if the latter had been the case.

Luciano noticed the question written on Nina's face and explained, "It's my uncle. He got a heart attack."

"That's awful." Compassion tinged her voice.

Luciano made no further comment on it. Instead, he dialled his grandfather and while waiting for him to pick up, he asked Nina to get dressed and alert the guards they would soon leave.

Luciano and Nina weaved their way through the brightly lit hospital corridors until they arrived at the coronary care unit. There, they spotted Nero standing as straight as a pillar, vigilant blue eyes scanning the area.

"How is he holding up?" Luciano asked his cousin.

Nero gestured to walk into the room behind him. "Take a look for yourself," he said while his line of eyesight shifted to the elderly man walking up to them.

The tapping of the cane had come to a stop. Nicolò removed the fedora hat and tucked it in between his upper arm and side, his combed back ash-grey hair showing clearly now. Combined with his wrinkle-free pinstripe suit, he didn't look like he had come in a rush.

"Did you come alone?" Luciano asked his grandfather.

"Sadly, no. But maybe when I leave?"

Luciano tilted his head. "Yes, maybe."

Nicolò ushered everyone into the room before telling his body-guard to stay put. He closed the door for privacy and embraced his daughter, Stella.

"It's getting more and more cramped in here. Look what you did, Nero. I told you to wait 'til tomorrow morning to tell everyone," Raniero grumbled.

Nero wasn't in the slightest fazed by his father's sour mood. "Technically, I didn't tell everyone. Only Luciano."

"Don't try and aggravate him, Nero," Luciano said in a stern but low voice.

He simply replied, "It's the truth."

Nicolò pushed a chair back and seated himself on it. "But how did this happen? You were looking good last time I visited you."

"I have my son to thank for that." Raniero huffed while new lines appeared on his forehead. "I ask him when he's finally going to get married. Here's what he tells me, 'On my wedding day,' the audacity of this kid blows the brain out of my goddamn mi-"

Nero shook his head, openly disagreeing with his father. "It's your own fault. You smoke and drink too much. Your eating habits aren't great either. You're in here," Nero's voice raised in volumed at the last part, anger filling him. "Because you're choosing that stuff over your family."

"You are far too young to talk to me like that." Raniero pointed a stern finger at Nero.

"Oh, so now I am too young? Isn't that convenient? You always say I'm too old whenever marriage gets brought up," Nero said, his ears turning a shade of red.

"Your father is bedridden and this is how you talk to him?" Raniero turned to look at his wife. "It's because you're too easy on him, Stella."

Nina side-eyed her husband, hoping he would step in and separate father from son to avoid further escalation as she was not in any place to do it herself. To her surprise, Luciano's main concern did not lie with his uncle and cousin, but with his grandfather. The ghost of a smile took shape on him and his eyes moved from Nicolò to her.

"I need to take care of something real quick. You need to stay here but if you need to go to the bathroom, or something like that, take Nero with you."

"Okay," she said, nodding her head.

No questions were asked.

Even though they did exist in her head. One of them being: what could he possibly have to do at a time and place like this?

Before Luciano exited the room, she saw him exchange a few words with Nero and guessed he told him the same as her – if not more. It seemed that Raniero and Nero would breathe the same air; the opposite of what Nina was hoping for. Avoiding conflict was always more favourable to her and even more so when one party couldn't allow being in a heated fight. While she didn't need to go to the bathroom, she still planned on going and have Nero tag along with her. Just to avoid a gnarly situation.

Luciano shut the door, greeted his grandfather's bodyguard and halted in his tracks.

"You don't happen to be a smoker, do you?" he asked the soldier.

"I am, Don."

"Would you mind if I borrowed your lighter and pack?"

The soldier's eyes widened. "No, of course, not." He handed his cigarette pack and lighter over to his Don.

"Thank you. I'll return them later." He tucked them inside his jacket. "Tell me where you parked the car. Lot or ramp?"

"Parking ramp, Don. First level and behind the fifth column." The soldier was hesitant in asking, "Was I not supposed to?"

"No, this is even better."

Luciano stepped outside the hospital, the automatic double doors sliding shut behind him. The dark sky of the city swallowed most of the view. He took a cigarette out of the crumpled up soft pack, lit it up and went to stand by the litter bin to tap the grey onto the ashtray.

This really is disgusting, Luciano thought as he made the orange light flare up again.

Whether he liked it or not, he had to look as if he simply came outside for a smoke. And not to hunt down the Irish soldier following his grandfather. This way, Luciano was able to take his time looking for the soldier and not risk alerting him so he could run away.

The Don's eyes searched the area and found the face he had burned in his memory. The Irish man pretended reading the newspaper on the bench.

He held it upside down.

Definitely not the sharpest tool in the shed.

The Irish soldier froze in his movement. He finally noticed Luciano was watching him.

Took you long enough.

Not a second passed by and the man began putting distance between himself and The Outfit Don. Fear seeped into him. The predatory glint in Luciano's gaze was enough to make him break out in cold sweat.

Luciano dropped the cigarette butt on the ashtray and stalked after him. They neared a steep ramp leading into the underground parking. It was a good place; far fewer prying eyes and only camera surveillance to worry about. Finding a blind spot shouldn't be too hard.

When the man was on even ground again, he began making a run for it. The action supplied Luciano with a slow smile tugging on his lips. He sprinted after him. Columns blurring on either side until he got to the ninth.

"No, you're not," Luciano said under his breath as he stopped the soldier from entering the black car by yanking him at the back of the jacket and holding him in a deadly chokehold. "I'll loosen my hold so you can breathe but one mistake on your part and you're dead."

A struggling groan came out of the man's mouth.

Luciano did as said, allowing the man to breathe. "There is something you need to do, Dean."

The Don knew his name. A tremor shook through the Irish soldier. His body froze and became completely speechless.

"Tell Banion to get his filthy dogs off my streets. Do that, Dean, and maybe, just maybe I won't skin you alive next time I catch you sniffing around my grandfather." Luciano warned.

The light of the low ceiling flickered above their head. A feeling of eeriness passing. Luciano tightened his hold, making the Irish man pass out. Though, it didn't take long for Dean to regain consciousness as Luciano malformed his hands.

The horrific fate led to Dean's scream to echo throughout the space.

The soldier's pointing and middle fingers were quickly discarded off by Luciano. He turned his back on the kneeling soldier and hid the bloodied knife under his clothes.

18

CHAPTER 18

The humming of a song ceased at the feel of Luciano's clean cuffs, the fabric comfortably hot from the iron. Last time she had seen the dress shirt, blood soaked the white into a red. Nina shook the memories away from that night at the hospital. She continued hanging the other ironed clothes on the rack and sang to the music playing in her head.

Nina had a good idea about what occurred during their hospital visit. After all, ever since, the streets had been quiet without a single Irish soul prowling around.

"You never fail to let me know where you are."

Nina snapped her mouth shut as soon as she heard him and prayed for her blush to die out.

I want to disappear. Forever if possible. More importantly, what is up with his timing? Does he have some sort of radar that tells him when I sing and snort like a pig?

"How else are you supposed to find me in this maze of a house? I do it on purpose."

Luciano left the door of the dressing room open, moved to stand next to Nina and put his heavy watch with the rest of his collection.

"Is that so?" he said with a faint lilt. "Is your blushing also on purpose? Because if so then I applaud you for it."

Nina returned her focus on sorting her husband's clothes, not wanting to indulge in his attempt to make her feel even more flustered. Instead, she casually remarked on how early he had come home. Nina began turning her head to face him but suspended the movement when she saw him undressing.

Toned muscles. Dark hairs dusted on his chest. Veins snaking down his arms.

"Yes, I am," he drawled and threw his black dress shirt on the pearl-grey ottoman bench. "Do you want a greeting kiss?"

The fingers on Nina's chin demanded she looked at him. His tone conveyed his suggestion to be half-hearted, just like every other time he proposed they do anything remotely sensual. Always expecting the answer to be the same. No. Luciano's body language betrayed the front he put up. It could easily be overlooked but he had turned toward her, his head tilting by a margin to catch her flowery scent.

Nina's heart fluttered in her throat, her cheeks once again warming. Her voice seemingly trapped inside her mouth.

"You do," he said as he noticed the cracking of her mask. Luciano diminished the empty space between them and let his touch trail the outline of her jawline. "Then what's holding you back? You already did it once before."

I'm not sure. What do I even look like through your eyes? You look disappointed with me. Am I right? I know I'm not what you want me to be but I don't know how to change. I don't know where to begin. I'm a failure – one with no spine but pretend to have one.

His left arm rested against the wall, supporting his weight and partly trapping her. "You're quiet, Nina."

When the skin around her jaw became colder and her throat heated, Nina's breath hitched. Luciano's hand acted as a velvet band; heat searing into her from the contact. While his grip was loose, he could still feel her swallowing.

"What do you want me to say?"

"You should know by now." His caress shifted to the valley between her breasts and ended at her waist.

The movement was slow and charged – excruciatingly so. Tingles spread around the places he had touched her.

"I don't think my thoughts will pique your interest."

"I'm sure they will."

"I'd prefer not to waste your time with them."

A low laugh passed by his lips, completely and utterly devoid of any mirth. "Whatever it is that is going around that pretty little head of yours, you're doing it to yourself."

And Nina was painfully aware of that fact.

Be honest. You need to be more open to him.

"What do you think of me?" she voiced one of her thoughts.

Say I'm anything but a disappointment. Please.

He arched a brow at the question but answered nonetheless. "Sweet, polite and smart." The colour of his irises bled into a darker hue of grey as a shadow cast over them. The muscle along his jaw ticked. Suddenly, he fisted the material of her clothes and pulled her closer. "You also have a talent to frustrate me to no end."

In an instant, Nina gathered the crumbled bits of her mask and glued them back on.

He added, "With every step we take forward, you take two back."

"I can work on that." How? She didn't know yet. She showed him an overly sweet smile and her tone was polite, "I should let you go now. You probably have a pile of work to do. I can go and heat dinner up if you want?" Needing to escape his presence, she brought her hand to his so he'd let go.

Luciano returned the gesture with his own tight-lipped smile. "Sure."

Nina was keeping herself busy in the sunroom by arranging the bold-coloured freesias. The mint-like scent of the horn-shaped blossoms reducing the anxiety inside her. She placed the vase at various spots, trying to see where it would look best.

A couple of hours ago, Giorgio texted that their father would make her cell phone ring.

Nerves had been creeping up on Nina like tiny insects. From time to time, she glanced at the phone sitting on the gold-plated edge of the salon table. She treated the device as if it was a ticking time bomb.

Ring.

Nina's stomach twisted and turned, creating knots in it. She dragged herself to the glass table and picked it up. Giorgio's prediction had been correct.

Ring.

The first call she had gotten from her father since marrying. A whole month.

At the third and final ring, Nina accepted the call. "Yes, Papà?"

"You have to come to New Orleans. Your uncle, Rino, died last night. His funeral is going to be held in a week," Carlos spoke as if he talked about the weather, very matter-of-fact.

Her eyes blinked in shock. It took a second before she replied back, "I don't know what to say."

"I can imagine."

"I'll tell Luciano when he gets home."

"Don't strain yourself. Do you think I haven't informed him already?" Carlos laughed at his daughter. "Fret not. Your silliness does have its charms, Nina."

The condescending tone he spoke in made Nina clench and unclench her hand. "What did Luciano say?"

"That I'll see you in two days. Anyway, I have work to do. We can catch up when you're here."

The phone was no longer pressed against her ear and got put back onto the table. She went to sit on the loveseat, staring at her phone in front of her.

These men keep confusing 'he died' with 'he got brutally murdered'. Nina released a soft sigh. Natural causes sure isn't what ended his life. Giorgio did say things have been rough over there. My best bet is that it's The Irish Mob. Her eyebrows knitted together when she seconded the thought. But didn't Luciano say they weren't as active over there?

What am I thinking? That doesn't matter right now. I should be calling Rosaria.

Nina had witnessed how her cousin's relationship with her father had been nothing short of a disaster but even then, Nina couldn't imagine her cousin not feeling a thing about her father's death. After all, he was still her father, right?

Come on, pick up, Rosaria.

She sighed softly at the ignored calls.

Nina's heart jumped at the slamming of a door. The front door to be exact. It was pretty early for her husband to return home. Curiosity pulled her toward the living room and recognized the male voices. Luciano and Nero.

"Let them reschedule the funeral because timing-wise it doesn't work out for me," Nero grumbled.

"Why don't you give them a call then?" Luciano's tone dripped in sarcasm as he held his phone out.

Nero looked at his cousin with dry amusement. "Ha ha."

"This doesn't change anything. You'll go to Philly without me."

"And what ab-" Nero stopped mid-sentence as he spotted Nina at the other end of the room. Realizing she must have heard everything he said, he offered her a gentlemanly apology for his foul speech and his condolences.

The latter was not necessary, in Nina's opinion, but she still accepted it. A weird look would be thrown at her otherwise. The grim reaper had visited her uncle. She had to act sad – at least, for as long she was in Chicago where people didn't know how sick the man in the head was.

Nina's gaze slid to her husband and found him looking her way. "Could you spare a minute?" she asked sweetly, stepping toward the sunroom so they had some privacy.

Luciano followed her shadow and closed the door behind him. "What is it?"

A slow smile tugged on her lips and she erased it before spinning on her heel to face him. She liked how he didn't offer his condolences. What she didn't like was that he could see through her false display of grief.

"At what time did Papà call you exactly?"

"In the morning." Luciano sighed and ran a hand through his hair. "I would've told you if it was before I left the house, Nina."

Disappointment sat like bricks on her shoulders. "I know you would."

Realization struck Luciano. This wasn't about when he told her the news. It was about when her father told her the news. He gritted his teeth wondering why his wife even bothered caring about her neglectful father.

Luciano stalked closer to his wife and rubbed the non-existent lines between her brows away while his own deepened. "You're going to give yourself a headache."

19

CHAPTER 19

New Orleans

The picturesque garden of Nina's old home was in pristine condition. Hedges and shrubs had been neatly trimmed. Weeds were nowhere to be seen. Blossomed buds were dotted throughout the place. The humid air was breathed in by Nina as she fell back into the good memories of her old life.

"Dad made sure it stayed the way you left it."

At lightning speed, Nina brought her hand to her heart before she spun around. She mentally rolled her eyes seeing it was only her brother. Of course, Giorgio would do the same song and dance with her. She didn't bother pretending to be mad at him for scaring her and went in for a warm hug.

"A hug right off the bat? Are you on your period?" A boyish grin showed on his face.

Nina lightly shoved him. "Fuck off!"

"Oh, cursing? That's strike number one."

"Shut up, Giorgio."

"Language, Nina. That's two already. You're doing good."

Nina laughed, shaking her head at him. She missed having these nonsensical conversations with him. Attentive eyes scanned her brother's appearance; he sported a crew cut which was much shorter than it used to be and had gained muscle on him.

"Is there someone you're trying to woo over?" She squeezed his arm.

Giorgio's lips curled downward. "What? No." He touched the ends of his brown hair. "I want everyone to take me seriously. Long hair isn't going to cut it."

"Is it working so far?"

"Fuck no. Those cocksuckers still think I'm a kid."

"Does that include Papà?" She arched a brow. "And why didn't you tell me he started going grey."

"He is?"

"Did you not notice? It's" – she drew a circle at the hair near the temples – "mostly this area. Not much but it definitely wasn't there when I left."

"Well, it's not strange. Dad and Mom are doing even worse." Giorgio noticed Luciano coming their way, his expression souring and his eyes rolling. "Great and now he's here."

That's it. I'm a hundred percent sure. He has a magical radar that tracks my voice.

"He's not that bad."

"Sure he isn't. Next thing you're going to tell me is that not all marriages end badly. I'm going. You can find me on the other side of the world." Giorgio left via the path on the side of the mansion in order to avoid bumping shoulders with his brother-in-law.

Irritation showed on Luciano's face and it was only to be expected. An hour into arriving at his in-laws and he could already feel his ears bleeding. He hated hollow pleasantries, small talk and prying eyes. The mere presence of Carlos chafed at Luciano's nerves and Evelyn was only bearable as long as she kept her mouth shut – which wasn't often.

"You pay too much attention to them."

"And what do you suggest I do?" Luciano said as he met up with her under the wooden archway.

"Do what I do."

He turned his head sideways, facing her and smiled – sort of. "That's not very helpful advice. You're telling me to either tune them out or take everything they say to heart. It's contradictory, not to mention ridiculous."

"You are putting words in my mouth again and that is not what I do," her tone as calm as the sea.

"I disagree."

She sighed softly. "Then what do you want from me, Luciano?"

He eyed his wife, taking note of how the afternoon sun kissing her eyes made them appear lighter. Luciano found them to resemble polished amber, yet at the same time thinking they were clouded.

"More than I thought I wanted," traces of wonder and frustration lingered in his voice.

Her lips slowly tipped upward. "That's quite cryptic."

For some reason, his words lay heavy on her despite not knowing what he truly meant.

"It feels that way." He averted his gaze away from her and peeked in between the vines to see glimpses of the Italianate mansion. This time around, he drank in the sights where Nina had spent all her life in and tried imagining what her childhood was like. "I didn't ask but were you close to him? Your uncle I mean."

"If this is about you considering to offer your condolences then don't. I don't mind it one bit. That man was an absolute creep. He's better off dead."

Luciano took in the unapologetic expression on his wife. Not once had he expected her to be this foul-mouthed. "You're not supposed to speak ill of the dead," he said despite finding her unfiltered thoughts immensely refreshing.

"I don't care much for that phrase. Especially in this case, how do you expect me to speak well of someone who has never done good."

"If I had known about your disgust toward Rino, I would've arranged it so that you could personally dig his grave – since you already have the needed experience."

Nina looked over at him while wearing a slight frown and only upon seeing Luciano smiling, she realised he was joking. "You had me there for a minute." She let her own smile broaden up a bit. Reflecting back on the last time they had spent time together in her old home, she wouldn't have predicted she'd be speaking this openly with her husband. Sure, Nina was a naturally hopeful person but even that had its limits given the circumstances.

This is nice.

"What is it? You've gone quiet again."

"I was just thinking that this is rather nice."

Just as Luciano opened his mouth to comment on it, his mother-in-law chose that moment to interrupt them by shouting Nina's name from inside the mansion, her hand waving them to come over.

"Yes, Mamma?"

"We have some serious catching up to do, Nina!" Evelyn said, then faced her son-in-law. "Moreover, I don't think you're a man who is wasteful of his time. Am I right or am I right?" Evelyn's gleeful laugh threatened an unwanted emotion inside Nina to boil to the surface.

"Actually, I promised Luciano to show him around town." She plastered on a lovely smile as she lied through her teeth and held him by his arm.

Luciano lowered his gaze to catch Nina's and for the first time he could clearly, without a shred of doubt, tell how she was feeling on the inside. Anger; but more than anything she felt hurt. It didn't appear as if Evelyn realised the effect her words had on Nina. Not overthinking his own actions, he signed himself up to be her partner in crime.

"It's as you heard, Mrs. Sciacca."

Evelyn wasn't given the chance to react as Nina steered Luciano away from that spot, disappearing into the path along the right side of the mansion. Once they were around the corner, Nina let go of Luciano and hid her smile behind the back of her hand before returning to her usual demeanour.

That felt good. But to think I'm glad to have him on my side feels strange.

"You're welcome by the way," he drawled.

"I call it a win-win situation. It's not as if you had nothing to lose or should we go back and then you can spend some quality time with my father? We all know how much you would love that."

Stunned by his wife's lack of filter, he simply followed her shadow as his eyes sparkled with amusement. They reached the front of the mansion and strolled over to Bartolomeo and Orlando who were taking a smoking break below the large tree with contorted branches. Seeing the two soldiers stand right next to each other caused Luciano to be more understanding of Nina's doubt in Bartolomeo's ability when she first came to Chicago. Physically speaking, Bartolomeo and Orlando were truly opposites of each other.

"So where are we going?" she asked Luciano.

"It's your city, you lead the way."

"In that case, we are leaving the car here. I'll be right back." She went inside her home and returned with a small handbag.

Luciano gestured the two soldiers to follow them before taking the spot beside his wife. "We're just going to walk with no destination in mind?"

"No, you'll see in a little bit."

They walked down the street until Nina pointed at a yellow sign, informing the Chicago men it was a streetcar stop and crossed the street. Soon enough, the St. Charles Streetcar appeared and slowed down before coming to a full stop, allowing the group of four to board the fern green vehicle.

"I've never been on one."

Nina heard Luciano's mumbling but made no further comment on it despite liking that she had introduced him to something new.

"Can I get four one-way tickets, please," Nina said to the conductor as she handed him five dollars.

"All righty! Here you go."

"Thank you." Nina distributed the white tickets amongst the men and made her way to an empty seat.

"You didn't have to pay for mine, Ms. Sciacca," Orlando spoke, bringing about Luciano's glare. "I meant to say Mrs. Gallucci. Force of habit."

"How about you just thank her?" He clapped him on the upper arm with a forced smile. "You stay in the front. Bartolomeo, you watch the back."

A sneer was visible on Orlando but the emotion was discarded for a more favourable one. "Thank you for the ticket, Mrs. Gallucci." He bowed his head to Nina and continued to do his guarding job.

Nina moved to sit by the window but was stopped by her husband. Instead, he went to fill up the window seat and had her sit beside the aisle. She raised an eyebrow, telling him nobody was going to try and snipe them.

"You never know." Vigilant eyes swept over the many heads inside the trolley. "And thank you for paying but don't they have one-day tickets?"

"They do but it'll be cheaper this way and you're welcome."

"Yes, because we're so tight on money." His sarcastic remark went flew past Nina's ears as she was too focused looking at the lively outside scenery. "Where exactly are we going?"

"You'll see," she said and although the smile on her lips was small, the one in her eyes twinkled with excitement.

Returning to New Orleans seemed to have a positive effect on his wife and Luciano wasn't sure why. According to him, it sure as hell wasn't her family who she was glad to be reunited with – her brother being the sole exception.

"You've changed," his voice drew Nina back in. "Or maybe you've always been like this, I don't know, but you are acting differently."

Nina stayed silent as she gathered her thoughts, trying to come up with an answer to his silent question. Why? "I guess I'm a little tired," she simply replied despite wanting to dive deeper into the topic. It wasn't the time nor place to have a conversation about her internal conflicts.

Upon entering the French Quarter, the group of four got off the trolley and had to do some walking until they reached the French

Market. Surrounded by a sea of people, Luciano tightly held Nina by the hand as to not get separated from each other.

A sense of nostalgia washed over Nina as she saw the many stands and familiar vendors. "I used to come here a lot when I was little."

"Really?" He sounded sceptical. "With whom? I can't picture Carlos going grocery shopping and I won't even mention your mother."

"Most of the time I came with my Nonna." A sigh of longing came out of her. "You know, there was a time when my father would carry me on my shoulders and read bedtime stories. He wasn't always like...how he is today. I suppose everyone deals with stress in a different manner."

Once again, Luciano chose not to voice his opinion about her defensive nature when it came to her father. He didn't even want to begin to understand. If it were him in her shoes, he would have cut ties a long time ago.

"What was yours like?" she asked in a gentle voice due to it being unknown territory.

"Good."

"That's all?"

"He was a good father to me and Teodoro and a good husband to my mother."

"Did you resemble him?"

"You're on a roll, aren't you? If you try picturing a younger version of Nicolò, you should have a pretty good idea as to what he looked like. There is a whole photo album in the library if you're curious."

"He sounds like a true family man."

"Yes, he was."

As much as her husband had indulged her in answering her questions, there was now a quality in his voice forcing her to stop. It was fine. His heartfelt declaration was more than enough.

20

CHAPTER 20

The guestroom in the Sciacca mansion was filled with a comfortable silence as both occupants went about their morning routine.

"Do we have any plans today?" Luciano asked his wife when he finished making up their bed.

"I'm going to my aunt and cousin. Do you want to come?"

"Will they give me a headache?"

"No, they are nice people."

"If you say so and you're sure they are free? Does your aunt not have their hands full with tomorrow's preparations? I imagine there will be plenty of people paying their respects at Rino's funeral."

"Papà said that pretty much everything had been taken care of. I'm sure he did so with pleasure."

Noting the dark tone in her voice, he said, "Your father also hates your uncle? Is it some sort of tradition that every male in your family antagonizes their brother-in-law? Tell me what Rino did."

It took her a second to process his words. In the past, he had never cared about or at least shown interest toward anyone outside her immediate family and she wished he hadn't started now.

"Do you really want to know?"

"Asking me that isn't going to make me less curious. So, yes, I want to know."

"I can't even begin to summarise the horrid things he did to my aunt. I'm sure she hasn't even told me half of it." She let out a heavy sigh. "Rosaria would often call me lucky to have a father like mine and-"

"Rosaria?"

"My cousin." She clarified, then she hugged herself. "After turning sixteen, I would notice Rino looking at me. He'd get too close to me during festivities; have his arm around my shoulder, dropping his head on my lap when he was drunk, hugging me too long during goodbyes. It felt degrading. Oh, and he always reeked of alcohol. Usually, I was able to handle it by subtly pushing him off me but sometimes his grip was too strong and since I couldn't go and create a scene," – Nina rolled her eyes in annoyance – "someone else had come to my rescue."

His hands were balled into fists. Fury coming to the surface but no one to direct it at. Can't exactly kill a dead man.

Sensing the changing air around Luciano, she continued, "Can you keep everything I just said between you and me?"

Luciano simply nodded, knowing how prideful she was; he would never bring it up again.

When the door to their room got opened without warning, heads turned toward it; one had their eyebrows scrunched together and the other had them up in surprise.

"What did I tell you about privacy?" Nina scolded her brother immediately.

"I'm sorry! I forgot you weren't alone."

"You still have to knock even if it's just her," Luciano said to Giorgio, feeling mildly irritated by his lack of manners.

Giorgio shot a glare back at him. "Nobody asked for your opinion."

"You have some nerve, Kid." Luciano's smile was more like a baring of his teeth.

"They're hopeless," Nina mumbled to herself as she slightly leaned against the doorpost of the adjoining bathroom. "Giorgio, what did you come for?"

"I came to ask where a certain someone was but," – the palms of Giorgio's hands showed as he gestured at Luciano – "Looks like I already found him on my own. You have to come to the office. My father wants to speak to you."

"What does he want to discuss?"

"How am I supposed to know? It's you he needs to speak to, not me." Giorgio said as Luciano passed by him to leave toward Carlos' office. "For someone who is supposed to be a Don he sure does ask stupid questions."

Still being able to hear Giorgio, Luciano ran a hand through his damp hair. "I'm going to kill this kid one day."

He walked down the dimly lit hallway, the heel of his dress shoe clicking against the hardwood floor and causing the young maid to pause her dusting of the vase table. She looked like the curious type: eyes glancing everywhere, putting ears against doors, touching things that aren't hers. The maid's body language suggested she wanted to run as far as possible away from the Chicago Don, and that was exactly what she wanted to do until she got called by him.

"Where is your boss' office?"

"Over here, Sir." She pointed at the closed door beside her.

Luciano thanked the maid and went for two short knocks against the heavy door before letting himself in and closing it again.

"Wonderful. It's very good of you to not make me wait and waste time like some other people do. Take a seat, have a drink, make yourself comfortable." Carlos held up a single finger, quickly following himself up by saying, "Not too comfortable though." He chuckled softly.

Avoiding a prolonged stay, Luciano refused a drink and sat down so Carlos could get on with it and tell him what he was summoned for.

"One of my soldiers came to me yesterday. Does Orlando ring a bell? Young, strong-looking-"

"Yes, I know who he is."

"You shouldn't interrupt people."

Politely smiling at him, Luciano said, "I was hoping to save you some time."

"Right." It came out clipped. "To cut it short: Stop ordering my soldiers around. I want to keep things peaceful and for that to be possible, it's essential for everyone to know their role."

There were myriad of things Luciano wanted to retort with but for the sake of keeping peace, he replied with, "Of course."

Orlando was one of many men who had a big ego and pride that was easily hurt. Going to Carlos to complain was standard procedure for the young soldier.

"Oh and before you leave, tell Nina to come here."

Luciano twisted the doorknob only halfway as the order got him to pause. All of a sudden, there was a strong urge of wanting to protect Nina from her father. "Is there something wrong?"

"Can't a father miss his only daughter?" he said, smiling widely.

Whilst dissatisfied with the given response, Luciano exited the study in search of his wife and told her about Carlos' request after finding her in front of the vanity mirror.

Nina's heart drummed in her chest. She detested getting called into her father's study since it was home to many conflicts in the past. A headache was already beginning to form and she hadn't even said a single word. Neither of them had. All she knew was she had done something her father wasn't happy with. At least that was what he communicated to her.

She crossed one leg over the other, the squeaking of the old chair emphasizing the silence in the room. Nina preferred this sitting position as it made her feel more in control.

"Papà?"

"It's been a month." Carlos let go of the pen, intertwined his fingers, and leaned back into his large leather chair. "It's been a month and you can't even make your husband understand his place in my house."

Nina internally flinched at the boom in his voice. There was no doubt the maids had something new to gossip about. Clueless as to what her father was going on about, she stayed put and watched him pace back and forth in the room.

"He's not in Chicago, Nina. He is in our city. He can't just order my soldiers around as he pleases. Who does he think he is? And that tone of his, I don't like either. I don't know what his parents taught him but respecting his elders wasn't one of them."

"What do you want me to say?"

"I can't do all the thinking here, Nina." He scoffed then looked her dead in the eye. "You are his wife. You know him. Explain to him how things ought to be!"

"I thought you said men from Chicago can't handle a woman with a brain."

Carlos shook his head, brows frowning in confusion. "When did I say that?"

"A few years ago."

"I never said that. My God. Do you write down everything I say?"

It was rhetorical but she still answered him inside her head. Yes. Nina remembered everything he had ever said to her. All of it was archived. The best of it and the worst of it.

Carlos cemented himself in one place and sighed in frustration. "What happened? Did you become a mute in Chicago? It's like I'm talking to a fucking wall. Maybe my expectations of you were too high. What do you want me to say?" he repeated her earlier question in a mocking tone. "Can't you think for yourself? You're a woman use that to your advantage." His bitter tongue then mumbled, "Disappointing."

Her father's words made her feel impossibly small. Suppressed tears were going to melt through her mask as if it were acid. Nina rose from the chair, ready to let it slide and walk away yet her body didn't seem to correspond with her mind.

"Take that back," she said calmly, her eyes devoid of any emotion. "Please."

He leaned a little forward as if he didn't catch what she said. "What did just you say?"

Carlos' act of disbelief was all it took for Nina to burst into a state of uncontained fury. The maddening insecurities her father had managed to feed through the years had her temples throbbing and her heart bleeding painfully. If possible she'd throw all of them in Inferno.

The thread desperately keeping her composure in check had snapped.

"Don't act as if you don't know what you just said to me. This is all your fault. You made me like this. Me constantly asking men what they want to hear is because of you!" Nina shouted to the point where her throat started to hurt. "You wanted me to be obedient. I did what you asked of me – what you expected of me – and this is what I get in return."

Having his daughter shout at him caused Carlos to be in shock. Completely and utterly speechless. Never before had she raised her voice against him. No one in the family ever had.

"You don't love me, Papà. You only think you do."

The second she uttered those final words, Carlos hit her across the face. Hard enough to leave a red mark.

Nina brought her hand to her cheek. Brown eyes brimmed with angry tears and her heart raced at the cruelty. Her anger stemmed from sadness, strong roots had nested themselves in the continuous circle of being let down by her parents. Not thinking about the consequences, she hit him with the same amount of force he had used on her. Before her father could give as much as a reaction, she left the study, flinging the door shut in his face as he yelled out her name.

21

CHAPTER 21

Luciano regarded his mother-in-law as she slipped some alcohol in her tea. Coming back to his in-laws, he knew it wasn't going to be smooth sailing all the time. Then again, he wasn't exactly shy of stirring things up either.

"Jesus Christ. The morning hasn't even ended."

Evelyn looked up from the mug, eyes wide open. Embarrassment showed on her cheeks. "I wasn't-" she began but stopped to look around for any curious ears; there was an older maid cutting vegetables who appeared to be absorbed by her work. Evelyn lowered the volume of her voice, "I wasn't doing anything and watch your language. We do not use the Lord's name in vain."

Irony tinged Luciano's polite smile. "I apologise. My eyes must have been deceiving me."

Problematic – all of them.

"Apology accepted." She gave him a curt yet wobbly nod.

Luciano leaned in a little closer and took a whiff. "It's not a pretty look. You could spray some perfume to cover it but I doubt it will do much," he spoke with a demeaning tone of voice.

Looking severely offended and not having any of it, Evelyn stormed out of the kitchen. Now having made a scene, Luciano had the eyes of the old maid on him to which he simply conveyed an act of being as clueless to the situation as her.

"Look at that; she forgot her tea."

"Yes, you're right." She put the knife down. "I will bring it to her."

"That is very kind of you," he said, having no qualms about feeding gossiping parrots.

He glanced at the watch on his wrist. What's taking her so long?

Tempted to go upstairs combined with the impatience getting to him, he left the kitchen but then stopped in his tracks when he heard loud shouting. It was the familiar voice of his wife yet unrecognizable at the same time. A door slammed shut – the one from Carlos' study Luciano guessed. He climbed the stairs with a scowl and asked the young maid where Nina was once he reached the top.

"In your room, Sir." She nodded at the guestroom.

Luciano's gaze slid to the study door and made his first step toward it, knowing that Nina wouldn't need his support as she was the type to deal with problems on her own. She had done so in Chicago and this wasn't any different. The uneasy feeling grew with each step and before he knew it, he went to check up on his wife instead. There was no one in the room, he closed the door behind him and moved silently toward the ajar bathroom door. There she was. Her eyes closed and her hands placed on top of her chest as if she was trying to calm herself down. It didn't seem to be working since her breathing was far too rapid.

"Nina," wariness laced his deep voice.

She turned her head, appearing to have been caught off guard by his presence. Only now Luciano saw an angry red marring her left cheek. A bottomless well of rage flooded at the sight.

"I'm dizzy," she said in between breaths.

Luciano closed the gap, holding her by the waist and letting her lean on him. "You're breathing too fast," his tone was stern rather than calm, worsening the condition Nina was in.

"I'm trying." Nina gripped onto his jacket and tried to follow his advice, fully aware she was close to having a panic attack.

"You put too much weight on the things your father says. Ignore him."

She frowned at his thoughtless comment. "I can't."

He took in a deep breath to try and stay composed. "If this is about you trying to protect your parents or trying to get their approval or whatever it is that you want, stop trying to get it. Stop worrying about it. You don't need them."

"Don't tell me what to feel and what not."

"You don't need their approval, Nina!"

"I know!" She raised her own voice as tears clung to her lashes. "Luciano, I can't do this now. I want to sit down," she mumbled in a shaky voice while her vision got stained with small black dots.

They moved out of the bathroom to sit by the window and as per Nina's instructions, Luciano opened the window so she could breathe in the fresh air. It was a simple solution to calm herself down but it had done its magic in the past.

"It usually takes about ten minutes for my energy to return."

Luciano watched her slumped figure, doubtful of her reassurance.

Without any prompting from Luciano, a switch flicked and Nina let out everything on her mind. "I want to hate him. I do but I can't. I can't hate him. I've tried for so long." Her tears were released from her long lashes. "It's so tiring. So draining." She went silent for a couple of minutes, appearing to be lost in thousands upon thousands of thoughts. "I wouldn't be devastated if he died tomorrow but I just can't bring myself to truly hate him."

Luciano was able to understand where she was coming from. Family was everything despite it not being a bed of roses. However, his emotions and views on what a family should be like challenged his leniency toward Carlos and Evelyn.

They don't deserve her.

"I just thought- I hoped if I did what he asked of me that he would love me," her voice shaky as more tears stained her cheeks.

When Luciano lowered himself to be on eye level with Nina, she didn't hesitate to accept the shoulder he had offered to cry on. If she was honest with herself, it wouldn't have mattered whose it was. She was at her limit. What did matter, were the words her husband chose to follow up with.

"You're not going to like this but you need to throw away these unrealistic expectations. Hoping for your father to change is not going to happen." Luciano waited for her to say something in return but only heard her hiccups. "You already told me that you're not blind to the type of person your father is. I'm not telling you to disregard the Carlos you used to know – the one that showed you love. But I do want you to distinguish one from the other."

For a split-second repentance was seen on her visage for showing her vulnerability to him, then she processed what he had said. Separate the old version from the man he had become. Never before had she thought about it like that.

"I'll try."

"Good." He brought his head back, getting a better view of Nina's face and wiped her tears away. "Do you need anything? Glass of water?"

She shook her head lightly. "No, I just want to go away."

"Where to?" He raised an eyebrow.

"We said we'd go to my aunt, right?"

"Are you sure?" he asked and got the nod of the head in response. "Alright. Can you stand?"

"If you'll help."

Luciano held her by the waist as they headed downstairs, moving through the parts of the mansion where no eyes were present. He glanced at her every other second. No mask on her face. Maybe she didn't care anymore. Maybe she forgot to place one, but Luciano had no intention of reminding her.

After grabbing their coats and getting outside, Luciano ordered Bartolomeo to start the car. The raising of his voice caught Giorgio's attention. The hot-headed young man dropped his conversation with Orlando and strode over to them. Luciano mentally groaned in annoyance seeing the accusing look in Giorgio's eyes. It was always guilty until proven innocent.

Before Giorgio got the chance to speak, Nina promptly explained that the bruise wasn't there because of Luciano.

"Dad?" he spoke through his clenched teeth.

"This isn't an excuse for you to pick a fight with him."

Giorgio pressed his lips together and shook his head hard in disagreement. "What about you? Are you gonna do anything?" he said to Luciano.

"No," he answered while opening the car door for Nina and closed it when she seated herself. "Stay here. I forgot something. I'll be right back."

"Okay." Realising she might stay the night at her aunt's place, she told him, "That's right, you should bring some extra clothes with you in case we stay there a little longer."

Luciano turned to Giorgio, lowering his voice so Nina wouldn't hear. "Keep her here, will you?"

Giorgio was quick to catch on. An understanding formed between the two men. One stayed with Nina and the other went back inside to settle things with Carlos.

The heavy door was flung open with brute force causing it to come in contact with the wall and make Carlos glower at the intrusion. It wasn't entirely unexpected though. He more or less predicted Luciano would come for a second visit given their history.

"Who are you? Huh? Tell me! Who are you?" Luciano bellowed as he stalked toward Carlos and slapped the glass of whisky out of his hand. He roughly grabbed Carlos by the face – palm over the mouth and fingers digging into the cheeks until he felt bone – to stop his staring at the mess on the carpet. "You're not going to find anything interesting over there. What happened? Can't talk? You had a lot to say to my wife, didn't you?" He repeatedly jabbed his finger against Carlos' temple at a quick tempo.

"Stop that!" He swatted at Luciano's hand and moved backward.

Meanwhile, Luciano finally detected the bruising on Carlos his cheek, a pitiless smile forming as he came to the conclusion it had to have been there because of Nina.

"You can't even look at me." A look of complete incomprehension draped over Luciano's silver eyes when he took note of Carlos his guilt-ridden expression. A flare of anger showed as it reminded him how Carlos' treatment of Nina indirectly affected his own marriage to her. "Are you just now realising your mistake?"

"I don't need someone like you for that!"

"I'd keep that tone of you in check. You still owe me a favour from that bullshit you pulled on my wedding." Connecting his fist with the bruise, Luciano hit his father-in-law multiple times hard enough to make him stumble and would have fallen to the ground hadn't Luciano caught him by the collar. "From now on, you will start being a father to Nina or else you can say goodbye to your standing in The New Orleans Family. You might be Don Galasso's little brother but being on good terms with me is of more value to him. Understand?"

He watched Carlos gingerly graze his cheekbone, certain that there was at least a hairline fracture if not worse. Deciding to end the conversation on this final note, Luciano released his grip and turned his back to the seething figure of Nina's father.

CHAPTER 22

"Even at home?" Nina commented on her aunt's choice of clothing.

Noemi looked down at her clothes of mourning and sighed. "What can I say? Not everyone calls before knocking on my door."

"That's true, yes."

Rosaria rolled her eyes at her mother's need to keep up appearances. "Who are we even trying to fool?"

"Him." Giorgio pointed a finger upward.

"God?" Rosaria guessed making her cousin and mother burst out laughing.

"No, you idiot. Luciano," Giorgio said after he got his laughter under control.

"You're not fooling him either. He knows," Nina spoke up.

"I don't like him," Rosaria mumbled.

Nina nudged her cousin with the elbow while giving her a look and ready to tell her not to be prejudiced against him.

Giorgio lifted his shoulders before sinking into the couch. "He's not that bad," he said creating a look of pleasant surprise on his sister. "Look I'll be the first to admit that I was quick to judge him but he has his priorities straight and I can appreciate that as a man."

Perhaps once, Nina would have caught wind of Giorgio's change in attitude toward her husband. Alas, due to her inner turmoil, all of her perceptiveness seemed to have vanished in thin air. She didn't even stop to think Luciano had lied to her when he went back into the Sciacca mansion.

"Enough about him. I'm just happy you're back." Rosaria encircled her arms around Nina, hugging her tightly. "I can no longer bear Giorgio's endless ranting sessions now that he doesn't have you anymore."

"Sounds like you have it pretty bad, Rosy." Nina caressed Rosaria's black hair as if she were a delicate doll. "I'll take my leave so you can enjoy some more of it." She smiled then kissed everyone goodnight and slinked out of the main room toward the stairs.

Nina slowed down in her steps at the sound of Luciano's voice. She thought he had already gone to sleep. Opening the door to their bedroom, she found him on sitting near the opened window. Contemplating to thank him now or later for the support he gave her earlier that day, her brown eyes stayed on him a little longer than intended.

Luciano was the first to break eye contact. "No, nothing. It's just Nina," he said into the phone, hidden away from Nina's sight. His brows fell low, concealing the dismay in his eyes. "My grandfather wants you."

She took the phone he held out for her. "Hello?"

"Could you do this old man a favour?" Nicolò his voice sounded gruff. "Luciano isn't the same as usual when we talked. Keep an eye on him. And don't let him notice I asked this of you."

Nina smiled faintly at the last part. "Of course and good night to you too."

Nicolò laughed. "I told you, you would fit right into the family. Goodnight, Nina."

She ended the call and handed the phone back after her eyes did an up and down of Luciano. There wasn't a speck of dirt on his portrait. But Nicolò had proven himself to be accurate when determining the mental state of others so she trusted his intuition.

"I still wanted to thank you for today," her voice as soft as a cloud. "For staying relatively calm when I couldn't."

"You must be really out of it. I'm not calm at all."

Nina's brows drew together when she felt his hand cupping the back of her head and brought her closer until she could feel his warmth embracing her. She allowed herself to relax, her nose grazing the crook of his neck. There was a firmness to his grip. Almost comforting.

A touch of warmth. Neither knew who it was supposed to help release them of their vexations.

"Why?" Her hands were rested on his stomach, unintentionally acting as a light barrier between them. "I mean, one of us has to be."

"I don't see why."

"To stop the other from going on a rampage," Nina's voice tried to quell Luciano's longing for conflict.

The corner of his lips snuck up into a smirk. "There is no need to."

"Maybe not, no." Nina's features mirrored the one on her husband.

Luciano wasn't able to act harshly against Carlos – not as much as he wanted to. There were rules in their world. And he was not above their law. If all leaders acted with only their sole interest in mind, tyranny would become of it.

The Don was aiming for a different trajectory.

All families under the wing of The New Orleans Family had gathered in the City of the Dead for Rino Esposito's burial. The above-ground tomb of the Esposito family hadn't been well-maintained. Moss grew on top of the vault. No flowers had been placed for its previous occupant and all of the once light-grey stones had turned into a darker shade; dirt covering it.

A light breeze swept a couple of dark-brown strands causing a disturbance in Nina's view of the burial. Normally, she'd wear her locks into a sleek ponytail or a bun since it was a sombre occasion but now she had no intentions of doing what was appropriate or not. While tucking her hair behind her ear, her fingers brushed against the make-up-covered cheek. As always, she looked flawless; unlike her father. During the funeral ceremony, she figured out what her husband had done after seeing the gnarly bruise on her father's face. She knew her own hit packed a punch but was still in enough control to not let it get that bad. It had to be fractured; there was this sunken appearance to Carlos' left eye – no doubt he also had some vision problems.

In a way, it felt good to know Luciano had her back. It was confirmation of a partnership forming between them. Her husband might not have his way with words but he more than made up for it in his actions.

From the corner of her eyes, it looked as though Carlos stared at her. "You did that, right?" she asked Luciano.

"Yes."

Carlos glanced at his brother, Galasso, and found himself thinking how he had become too much like him. Rays of the sun shone across the amber of his daughter's eyes. The radiant colour reminded him of his late father. He wasn't sure why the thought popped into his head. Perhaps it was because of the abundance of death surrounding him. When Luciano caught him looking in their direction, he returned his focus on the burial. Nina would never know of the remorse living underneath his hardened gaze.

"How long are you staying here?" Arturo whispered to Nina.

"I'm not sure. Shorter than I planned on. Why?"

"My father plans on inviting you two for dinner at one of our restaurants once we're done here."

"Really? What for?"

"I think you can take a good guess," her cousin answered.

Of course. Get on our good graces. Now, he wants to play the nice uncle. Leech, her mind whispered.

"How many will be there?" Luciano asked this time.

"Ten – maybe more."

Luciano felt uneasy at large social gatherings – be it a celebratory event like a wedding or a dinner party consisting mostly of strangers, or even going to church. It wasn't always like this and while he had always been raised to be cautious, the feeling of unease was something relatively new. This sounded especially true now that he was in unknown waters.

"We'll see," Luciano said.

Arturo nodded in a polite manner and stepped away from the couple.

So far, no tears had been shed throughout the day. Albeit it being common for the men to not show any sign of vulnerability, it was socially acceptable for the women to do so yet they didn't. The man was detested amongst everyone. Even his own mother couldn't bring herself to cry. Thick grey locks framed her face as she stood with Rosaria and Noemi – all of them having had their own fair share of Rino's oppression.

Tempted to check the time on his watch, Luciano lifted his arm ever so slightly.

"They are almost done," Nina informed him.

When Bartolomeo moved from his spot at the entrance of the cemetery and toward his Don, several curious eyes tracked his movement. A phone was against his ear, a dire look etched into his visage and there was a hurriedness in his pace.

"For you, Luciano," he said hushed.

"Who is it?"

Bartolomeo shook his head, his eyes moving around in paranoia. "I don't know. Some guy just handed it to me and said I should give it to my boss."

Not liking the sound of it, Luciano told Bartolomeo to stay with Nina and proceeded to move away from the crowd but still close enough if she needed protection.

"This is Luciano."

"Congratulations on becoming Don, Luciano. It's Cillian."

Luciano's lips shared similarities to a dead man's heartbeat on a monitor as he continued listening to the head of the Irish Mob.

"Have you seen the news lately? They say lots of rats have been crawling around North Side. Ah, well, it makes sense. Rats have to eat too, you know. It's a prosperous place. Lots of restaurants, so many dumpsters full of food."

"Get to the point, Banion."

"And there is uh- this stench...this godforsaken stench hanging in the air that I've been trying to get rid of. I'll let you in on a little something: I have a theory that they all came from South Side

Chicago." The tone of Cillian's voice shifted into a sinister one. "To give back to the community, I thought to clean them all up."

The unwanted emotion of human fear settled in as Luciano recalled a night of great loss. Anything but a repetition of the night from four years ago.

This time around, Chicago wasn't the only city under fire.

Luciano had no time to dwell on the past as lead rained down in the City of the Dead. Chaos blanketed over everyone within milliseconds as they heard the screaming of a semi-automatic.

23

CHAPTER 23

The Irish didn't pull back their punches and brought war into the homes of the Italians. Not even the deceased were left alone.

The families sought cover behind the many mausoleums at breakneck speed from the bullets. Doing what he did best, Bartolomeo acted as a shield for Nina and had his gun drawn as his eyes searched for the enemy.

Nina was crouched down, her hand against the stone of the tombs, and looked around for Luciano. She found him. He was still out in the open causing fear to pulsate through her veins. Frightened to see his body be riddled with lead. A phone slipped out of his hand, a gun taking its place and he sprinted toward her.

The round of fire came to a stop.

"Don't move. Are you okay?" Luciano said, his gaze checking if Nina had any injuries. There were none.

"Yes." The word was almost stuck in her throat. "You?" she asked to which he gave a curt nod.

"Stay here." Carlos held Nina by the arm and could feel her trembling. "Where is your mother?"

"I don't kn-"

Another round of fire reached everyone's ears. Hopeless terror engulfed the youngest of minds present at the shoot-out. Fresh blood coated the cemetery grounds. The onslaught seemed to last forever in Nina's mind even though it happened in a matter of seconds in real-time.

When the roar of a car's engine sounded, Luciano looked carefully around the corner of the mausoleum while Carlos and Bartolomeo checked the other side. Banion's men left and the chase would begin.

Luciano made eye contact with Bartolomeo, the experienced soldier ready to take orders. "Take Nina to the mansion!"

"Wait! Don't go, they are long gon-"

Nina was cut off by Luciano giving her a hasty, yet intense last kiss. Too high on adrenaline and too much in a state of shock, she did not register any pain as he grabbed her roughly by the face. All of it felt numb. She only got a brief look of the terrifying rage flashing across her husband's face before he went after The Irish with Arturo and Giorgio.

Don Galasso barked orders that every man bring their wife and children to safety and hunt the enemy afterward.

There wasn't any time to process what was happening. It was one thing after another. Now, it was Nina's mother. She had been hit in the arm.

"Papà, come!" Nina ran toward her mother. "Put pressure on it, Mamma." She unknotted the silk scarf from her neck and wrapped it tightly around her mother's arm to put pressure on it so the blood would clot.

"Do something," Evelyn breathed out and held onto her daughter.

The firm grip on her arm was released when Carlos lifted her mother in his arms and got told to call their private doctor. Once they reached the car and got inside, Nina dialled the doctor. With her father trying to calm her panicking mother down, Bartolomeo took hold of the wheel and drove the family back to their mansion. Even though Nina didn't see a single scratch on her aunt and cousin, she still called them to check up on them and to her relief, they got away with only a scratch or two.

There were a handful of doctors The New Orleans Family had direct access to. Luckily, it didn't take long for Dr Sartini to arrive at the Sciacca mansion.

"I'm going to remove a small fragment but I can't do anything if you keep moving away. I need you to stay still. Can you do that, Mrs Sciacca?" Dr Sartini said, the professional tone of his voice having a calming effect on Evelyn.

Whenever a child of a mafioso excelled in a certain subject at school their father would push them to pursue a career in that field. Some became doctors, others lawyers, and some politicians – all of them eventually benefitting The Family in one way or another. Dr Sartini was once such a child.

Nina drew in a breath as her mother's iron grip tightened. She didn't mind it though, it anchored her. Otherwise, her mind would be frequently drifting off to Luciano. Where was he now? Did The Irish get to him? In what state would he return?

"It's for Mrs Gallucci," the maid directed her attention at Nina as she slipped into the living room with a telephone.

Carlos snatched the phone from the maid and promptly handed it to Nina. He turned his head sideways to face the maid again and spoke, "Since when does the help answer phone calls in this house?

If you hear a phone ringing, you pick it up and bring it to me before anyone else. Don't let me see you make this mistake again."

The maid was quick to apologise and left the room, not wanting to be exposed to her already agitated boss any longer.

Nina pried her mother's finger off of herself and signalled her father to give comfort in her stead. Once she was out of hearing range, she spoke to the caller.

"Hello?"

"Nina, where is Luciano? The girl said he wasn't with you."

There was something off about Nicolò his voice. It wasn't the steady tone she was used to hearing from him.

"He is- I don't know where he is. There was a shooting at the cemetery, Luciano went after the shooters and he- he hasn't returned yet."

"He'll be fine. You can trust him to be level-headed. But this is bad," It took a while before Nicolò spoke again, "The Bureau will be all over this. When he comes back, tell him there has also been one in Chicago."

A lump formed in her throat as she registered the magnitude of the attack. On top of having The Irish Mob exerting pressure on The Outfit and The New Orleans Family, the Bureau, with the help of the New Orleans Police Department and Chicago Police Department, would be suiting up for a more active role in their investigation against the criminal organizations. Two sizeable attacks in affluent neighbourhoods would not be overlooked by the officials.

The front door slammed open making Nina whirl around. A wave of relief fell over her at the sight of Luciano. Though the feeling was quickly washed away when she saw the bleeding figure of her brother whose arm was slung around Luciano's shoulders for support. He was shot in the shoulder.

"Call Dr Sartini!" Arturo shouted as he put pressure on the bullet wound.

"He's here," Nina was able to get out as she guided them toward the main area.

Everyone's eyes – except for Dr Sartini's – had been on the door even before they entered the living room. The urgency in Arturo's shouting had reached them as well. Carlos his lips parted in shock when he saw his son's blood trickling down his arm and fingers. It felt like his world was upside down.

The two men laid Giorgio down and Nina came to his side, telling him that he was going to be fine. That no one could hurt him now. Her eyes burned as she saw the pain Giorgio was in.

"Keep him awake. I'm almost done here," Dr Sartini said.

"No, please, go to him. I can wait," Evelyn said.

"When I say I'm almost done, Mrs Sciacca, I actually mean it. It'll take me less than a minute."

Nina lightly slapped Giorgio's cheek when she caught him closing his eyes. "Stay with me, Giorgio."

"I know, I know," he mumbled.

Dr Sartini moved over to Giorgio as he gave Carlos instructions on how to properly dress Evelyn's wound and began aiding Giorgio. Nina stepped back, making more room for the doctor, and jumped when Luciano placed his hand on her elbow.

"Come." He pulled her out of the main area and into a windowless part of the mansion.

"But-" Nina began retorting as she didn't want to part from her brother.

"Were you followed when you drove away from the cemetery?"

She shook her head, then dread knocked on the doors in her mind. "You think there will be a second attack."

"There might be. Until we leave the city, everything you do will need to be done with that assumption." He removed the brown strands of hair sticking onto her neck because of the sweat. Finally taking note of her paler skin tone, he said, "You're not well."

"No, but I'll be fine." She leaned in a little closer, seeking out his comfort.

It wasn't until he embraced her how much wanted her in his arms. Safe with him. To simply feel the skin to skin as he kissed her on the temple. "You're safe now."

Her hands moved to touch his back, then stopped, hovering in the air. Her lungs were bereft of oxygen as she remembered the call from earlier. Luciano didn't know yet. She stepped back, out of his reach, and deepened the creases in his features when she repeated Nicolò's words to him.

It was time for The Outfit Don to return to his city and get in touch with Enrique García.

24

CHAPTER 24

C hicago

    South Side Chicago appeared to be in hibernation. No wonder it was. Walking the streets left Nina speechless. Bullet holes riddled the scenery, yet the residents weren't shocked by it. They were used to gang violence.

"We'll go through the backdoor," Luciano said as they walked over patches of grass, moving around his uncle's house.

They were there to visit Felicia. She had to be bandaged up because of flying glass shards. Her young age did not exclude her from Banion's brutality.

From his peripheral vision, Luciano saw his uncle peeking between the blinds after he knocked on the door. His uncle's action was nothing to bat an eye at. Luciano was certain the man would have done the same thing even if the attack hadn't occurred. For the longest time, Luciano thought of his uncle as a paranoid man.

"Don't stand there! Hurry! I think it's going to rain soon." Orfeo waved them to come inside the house. His eyes locked onto the steaming casserole in Nina's hands, rubbed his hands together and said, "Oh, you didn't have to! You're lucky with a wife like her, Luciano. Let me free your hands of it, Nina. I'll bring it to the kitchen."

Stepping inside, Nina thanked him as she handed it over. Even when she and Luciano were left alone, she made no remark about Orfeo's attitude. It was surprisingly upbeat for someone whose daughter was hurt.

"Don't mind him. He's always like that."

"Really?" she asked to which he nodded.

Out of nowhere, three little girls and a boy appeared in the doorway leading to the living room. Apprehension flitting across most of their faces as they didn't recognize their older cousin. Some family members weren't as used to Luciano's visits as others.

"Where is your mother?" Luciano asked them.

"Upstairs with Felicia," the oldest of the bunch said.

"Why did you say that! No one can go there!" the other two girls yelled at her.

"Shut up!"

The hair pulling between the kids was quick to end as their father entered the room. Orfeo led Luciano and Nina to the second floor and toward Felicia's room.

Nina instantly recognized Felicia as the same waving and smiling little girl at her wedding. Now, the smile was robbed of the girl, and given to her were wounds. Sorrow chipped at Nina's heart to see her in this condition.

The manner in which Banion orchestrated the hit was void of honour in Luciano's opinion. He had no qualms about seeing blood from men and women flowing through the streets – in the middle of a war, it was only natural – but he did draw the line once it concerned innocent children. Even amongst the most wretched of men from The Outfit, that was unacceptable.

"Those were agents, weren't they? They followed us all the way from your uncle's home." Nina referred to the conspicuously parked car in the streets of Lincoln Park.

Luciano honked impatiently for the soldiers to open the gates to his home. It didn't take much to figure out what had gotten him like this. The Irish slipped out of his grasp in New Orleans and his own family had to pay with blood, the spotting of people from the Bureau was truly the rotten cherry on top.

"They were also there?"

"Yes, did you not see them?"

Luciano pressed against the gas pedal and mumbled, "I only started seeing them about five minutes ago." He ran his other hand over his face, muffling the curses slithering out of his mouth.

As frustrating as it was, his hands, as the Don, were tied. There was nothing he could do against the Irish while the officials kept him under tight surveillance. The new Don failed the family. Humiliating was one way to call it in his eyes.

They stepped out of the vehicle and toward the mansion.

"Have you received any news on your brother?" he asked suddenly.

"He's recovering, and says not to worry about him," she answered, surprised with his interest in Giorgio's well-being. "You can give him a call if you want."

"No, thank you."

They shut the entrance door behind them and separated ways. Each going about their own day. Luciano had to deal with the new situation and Nina made a few phone calls where she checked up on every Outfit family.

The clock's short hand moved across the face, yet Luciano's mood remained the same. Nothing could be done against his enemies. Everyone had to lay low and be even more discreet about business than before. He sat in his office and did what he did best; being a workaholic. These were stressful times but he couldn't afford to slip up.

"I think we should call it a night. You look like shit." Nero said.

Luciano glared at his cousin. "With which hat are you telling me this?"

"Both." Nero slung the door open then looked over his shoulder. "I mean it by the way, you really look like shit."

"Fuck you." He stretched the words out as he watched Nero leave with a broad smile.

Luciano walked out of the room and in no time at all, he found himself before his wife. There she was. In the sunroom like all the other times he had found her there. Luciano knew for a fact that she was aware of his presence despite her eyes not being on him. He shifted his weight to lean against the doorway and simply watched her reading a newspaper focused on financial matters. There was nothing he had to inform her of, yet his steps led him to her. Maybe he had to see if she was safe? Maybe he needed to see her because everything else about his future felt uncertain? Maybe he just wanted her company? He didn't know.

Curious brown eyes flitted over his face, then the ground he stood on, and returned to the papers. A soft exhale was heard. She must have sensed he wasn't going to say anything.

"Is there something you want?" Nina asked him.

"No." He stepped away from the doorway and drew closer to her. "I don't think so," he mumbled as he looked at the article.

"Do you do this? Virtual horse racing?" Nina angled the paper so he could read it.

"I've only heard of it." He pursed his lips as if in deep thought. "It's not a bad suggestion. I might look into it," he said while taking a seat in the armchair.

"You should. It could be a very lucrative investment."

Luciano made a mental note of it, taking her advice and noting how her words brimmed with confidence. Once again, he observed his wife. Not a single flaw to be seen in her posture, her back straight, her legs crossed, and her head held high as she immersed herself in the news.

"You keep looking at me," she voiced.

"I can't look at my wife?"

"It's distracting." She closed the papers and put them away. Nina turned to him, thinking to herself that there was something off about him. "You always do that. You always call me your wife."

"Yes," Luciano said as a faint smile appeared. "Or are you going to tell me that our wedding was a fabrication of my mind? Because I'm fairly certain it did happen."

"No, it was all a big dream," she said sarcastically to which he let out a chuckle. "But why? It's not as if you call me that out of endearment."

Luciano briefly looked the other way as mirth was quick to leave his expression.

Why?

In the beginning, I did it to remind myself. My wife. Someone who I was supposed to care deeply for.

Luciano hoped repeating it would help him better grasp that feeling; the way a husband was supposed to love his wife. His efforts were futile. Calling Nina his wife wasn't what got him to care for her.

Why ask this, Nina? Small talk never does it for you, does it?

"I'm not sure why I used to say it so much," he answered, not voicing his real thoughts as the truth would only cause pain. Words like these could very easily be taken the wrong way. "But I can tell you why I still call you that."

Nina held her breath as solemn onyx eyes glided from her face to golden band on her ring finger. She wanted the answer but didn't ask further. Traces of reluctance bled into his voice as he spoke. Nina rid herself of the tension in her muscles, her gaze softening and her posture less rigid.

"No, it's fine." Her eyelids felt heavy and so, she opted to go to bed a little earlier than usual. "I think I'll go to bed. Sweet dreams, Luciano."

Her voice floated in the air. A caress sweeter than nectar. He laid his eyes on her warm skin tone, wondering if it was as smooth as it looked – despite already having had a taste of it before.

He rose and followed her into the bedroom, stating how he was also in need of sleep. They crept under the covers, both on their own side of the large bed. Darkness draped the room as his wife pulled on the lamp's chain. Before long, he sat up, discontentment looming over his head as he looked at the wide gap between them. They might as well have been sleeping in separate bedrooms. Not thinking too much about it, he bridged the distance and snaked his arm around Nina's waist.

"Do you know that you drive me mad?" His breath fanned the sensitive skin of her neck.

"No," she answered.

Luciano turned her around, his grip firm, and met her awaiting gaze. "Do you truly mean that?"

"No," she breathed out.

The confession almost got him to hover over her smaller frame and adorn her flesh with marks.

If only I wasn't this goddamn tired.

25

CHAPTER 25

Nina turned the radio's dial, surfing through a range of channels until she came across an audio play she used to listen to as a kid. It was a mystery drama from the fifties. She leaned back in the chaise lounge and let her eyes rest on the dancing flames in the fireplace. The radio drama brought her mind back to New Orleans, and eventually, the feeling guided her to the time Luciano spoke about his parents.

She stepped out of the library and into the hallway, coming eye to eye with her husband as he shut the door to his study.

"I was just coming over," she said.

"For?"

She walked back into the library, leaving the door open so Luciano would follow after her. "Where is that photo album you talked about?" She went over to the never-ending row of spines on the many shelves.

Luciano crouched down, his finger skimming over the albums until he found the right one. "This one," he mumbled and pulled it out.

"Thank you," Nina said as she took the cotton white book from him. "Will you stay around to narrate?" The shimmer of hope in her eyes began to fade when he didn't answer right away. "Or are you tired?"

"No," he answered to her last question, moved over to the chaise lounge and gestured for his wife to come to him. "I want you here."

She didn't have to be told twice and she sat beside him, their knees brushing each other. But it wasn't close enough in Luciano's opinion and so, he shook his head and told her to sit sideways in his lap. He grabbed the bare skin of her legs – as her dress had slits – and had his other hand on her waist before adjusting her position.

"Are you comfortable?" he asked.

Both of them were fully aware that he only asked this to get a reaction out of her.

Nina scared her blush off and instead, she gave him a sweet smile. "Very."

Luciano's attempts at making Nina feel flustered would never cease. In a way, Nina was glad it never would. It was part of their routine.

The album was opened by Nina. Strangely enough, the first image was not a photograph but a detailed drawing. An array of emotions flowed through Luciano's veins and through his heart as he saw the depiction of himself and his family – joy as it send him to a place he hadn't visited in a long time, melancholy and anger as it was a reminder of what was taken from him, and worry as he had almost lost everything again with the recent terrors.

"Who drew this?" curiosity and awe tinged her voice as her finger touched the edges of the ink drawing.

Pride filled Luciano as he said, "My grandmother."

The drawing showed the Gallucci family in the garden of Nicolò's mansion. In the middle stood Nicolò, on his left was a young man, and on his right a young woman. The younger couple made Nina knit her brows until she realized it must have been Luciano's parents.

"Is this Teodoro?" Nina tapped on the boy in the young woman's arms to which Luciano nodded. "So, this must be you," she concluded as she pointed at the boy in front of the young man.

"Yes."

"What is your mother's name?"

"Giulia." Luciano moved on to the next page showing her a picture of his parents as newlyweds. "What? Not curious about my father's name?"

"It's Riccardo, right? I remember seeing it along with your and your uncles their name on the list." Her eyes slid back to the photo. "He does resemble Nicolò."

"In more ways than just their looks. They always took care of their family."

"Still do," Nina spoke up, correcting him to which he arched a brow. "Your Nonno still looks out for you."

"Oh really?" he drawled. "And how do you know?"

"Call it intuition."

"Nina," the rumble of his voice caused the fine hairs along her neck to stand up. "The truth."

The urge to obey his command was smothered by Nina, until Luciano made his next move. The grip on her waist grew firmer and his other hand steadily reached the outer part of her thigh, stroking it. Her name rang through the room, his voice, ever so slightly, lower than before. His scent drew closer as his head leaned in, the tip of his nose grazing her rosy cheek before his lips left a kiss near the nape of her neck.

"Tell me," he mumbled against her warm skin.

"I thought we weren't supposed to against our elders." Then, she released a soft sigh. "He asked me not to tell you."

"I'm your husband," his spoke in a low voice.

"He asked me to keep an eye out for you – said that you weren't like yourself. He sounded very worried about you, Luciano." Nina looked into his eyes. "What were you so tormented about?"

He frowned. "When was this?"

"After the-" She began but stopped to come up with a better answer. "The night we spent at my aunt's place."

"Oh." He stopped frowning. "Yes, it's coming back."

Wry amusement painted his features and his stubborn self wanted to seal his lips shut. Luciano wanted to eat his own words as it was only fair for Nina to play the same card he had used on her: I'm your wife therefore you have to tell me the truth.

"Is it really coming back?" she said to his silence.

"Right," he said with slow smile that was quick to fade as he relived that day. "What happened in New Orleans makes you remember what you've got to lose. I simply felt – or still feel – unsure about what is to come." He moved her hair behind her ear. "Things can change drastically in the blink of an eye. Now, you're in my arms, and next thing you know we're separated."

"I'm not going anywhere."

"I know."

"Don't say things like that then. You sound like some kind of ominous fortune teller."

"Do I, now?"

Nina placed her hand on the side of his face, the tip of her finger coming in contact with his scar. "You're worried the Irish are up to something again?"

"No. I'm not worried about anything right now nor should you." He flipped the page, wanting to drop the subject and get her attention elsewhere.

Nina's gaze remained on him as she did not believe him, and although she wanted to continue her questioning, she had hunch that Luciano didn't held any answers to begin with.

There came no end to the insistent ringing of the telephone and so, Serena stopped her task at hand and made haste to get the call to Mrs Gallucci, believing that the call was more important than she had initially assumed it to be. Outside, Serena found Nina, and Bartolomeo, raking dead leaves into several heaps.

"Mrs Gallucci, for you. They've been calling for a while now."

"Thank you, Serena." Nina accepted the call and walked away from everyone.

Giorgio's beaming voice greeted Nina. The call from New Orleans was foreseeable as it was her birthday. The phone got passed down until she was met with her father's voice; the one person she didn't expect to bother speaking to her at all. During the entirety of their conversation, Nina kept her voice monotone. While she did appreciate him making an effort, she would call his attempt at giving affection half-hearted at best.

"I'm going to hang up now and-"

"I'll give your greetings to Luciano, don't worry, Papà."

"You should've let me finish my sentence," Carlos grumbled. "Happy birthday, Nora."

The sound of her nickname had Nina end the call with a lump in her throat. It had been ages since her father last called her that.

Nina went inside through the sunroom to return the telephone and stumbled into Luciano on the way. Immediately, the lump crumbled into smaller pieces. She was safe with him. However it didn't stop her from putting on a good face before asking him about his day.

Old habits die hard.

"Good. I was looking for you." He glanced at the phone in her hands. "Your family called?" he asked to which she nodded. "And Carlos?"

"Yes, I also spoke with him." Nina tilted her head, wondering why he was so curious about it. "Why do you ask?"

"How was it?"

She lowered her gaze, thinking back on her old nickname. "Not that bad actually."

"That's good."

"It is. I mean, I don't plan on forgiving him but...it was good to hear from him." She gave him a small smile. "But why were you looking for me?"

"Don't you know? It's part of my daily routine." He reached into the inner pocket of his suit jacket and held out a gift, it was a small box with a swan on it. "Happy birthday, Nina."

"Thank you," she said, her words coming out carefully. She had trouble hiding her surprise as she wasn't expecting to get anything. She opened it, the box revealing a dainty necklace. "I'll take good care of it. Thank you again, Luciano."

"Your thoughts?" He arched a brow. "Do you like it? You don't have to be polite about it."

Nina let out a light laugh as she thought back on the first time he bought her jewellery.

"I love it."

CHAPTER 26

"Oh dear!" Serena exclaimed.

Nina followed the maid's line of eyesight, pushed the roller shades out of the way, and spotted her husband and Nero outside. The anger in Luciano's eyes was palpable enough to send chills along her spine.

Nero kept his distance as he talked to his Don. Apparently, Irish soldiers sauntered around at the horse race track. Grounds that unofficially belonged to The Outfit.

"Don't you fucking say they're not doing any funny business." Luciano dared Nero to speak against him.

"No, but this is not the time to do stupid things. Need I remind you that they are watching us even closer now." Nero said, knowing his cousin through and through.

Luciano shook his head, not wanting to listen to his consigliere, and opened the car door.

"What are you doing?" apprehension seeped into Nero's voice.

"Putting my foot down." Luciano slammed the door shut and drove away.

Luciano ripped his eyes off the rear-view mirror once he saw Nero was on his tail. Any other time, he would've at least listened to his advisor but lately, Luciano was high-strung – the smallest of inconveniences had him putting a strain on his vocal cords. It was one loss after another ever since that night. He stepped on the gas, wanting to get to the horse race track before any of the Irish soldiers were gone.

Those little shits think they're untouchable.

Once he reached his destination, he walked in strides toward the entrance and just then, the sound of screeching tires was heard in the background. Luciano didn't turn at it. He'd face his consigliere later on.

"Joe!" Luciano called out when he spotted one of his men.

The short soldier who informed him of the Irishmen hurried toward his boss. "They're right by the tracks, Don."

Luciano continued to walk down the shadowy hall while Joe was right behind him. From the corner of his eyes, he caught Joe fiddle with his fingers.

"Spit it out. What's wrong?" Luciano said.

"Uh...it's just that capo Orfeo and Paolo are already dealing with the situation. Won't we attract too much attention?"

The fierce scowl on Luciano caused the soldier to stitch his mouth shut and walk a few steps behind him.

"Joe," he said, making the soldier's ears perk up. "Nero will be here in a second and ask for me. I need you to lead him the other way."

"Yes, Don. What, uh, should I tell him?"

"Jesus Christ, make something up!"

Luciano stepped out into the sunlight, his eyes scanning the area before searching for his captains and the Irish soldiers. They were indeed right by the tracks. The group of four appeared to be in stalemate. The Irish soldiers their backs were unguarded as they were eye to eye with the Italian capos. One of the soldiers, Luciano knew all too well. The other one, not so much – comparatively speaking.

Luciano headed over to them, a look of delight veiling his face as if he was about to reunite with childhood friends.

Luciano slung his arms around the soldier and said, "I missed seeing you around, Dean. How is the hand?" Appal twisted into his features as he glimpsed at Dean's maimed hand. "That's not a pretty look. Did the doctors not help you out?" Luciano said in a mocking tone.

"We're not looking for a fight," the other Irish soldier said to Luciano.

Luciano eyed him. Hayden Banion, a nephew of Cillian. He remembered him as one of the more capricious men in the Irish Mob; as well as the man that kept sniffing around his mansion.

"Aren't you two birds of a feather?" Luciano's question to Hayden and Dean was rhetorical, yet his tone suggested they seriously answer him.

"No," Dean croaked out.

"They say Banion sent them to propose a truce," Paolo clarified to his Don.

Luciano slid his gaze to Paolo, his uncle and also one of the older captains in the family. As always, Paolo's medium-length hair was greased back and styled with utmost care. Luciano and his cousins would often call it an heirloom as they suspected it to be a toupee.

"You hear this guy? A truce," Orfeo scoffed.

Cillian Banion knew Luciano would not accept the offer. He was merely taunting the young Don; and it worked.

"You keep pushing your luck," Luciano said in a low voice. Luciano grabbed Dean by the back of the neck and craned it so he could see the observant FBI agents. "Don't think for one second they're your guardian angels."

Luciano slammed Dean's forehead against the white railing causing Hayden to spring into action. A groan came out of Luciano as he was tackled to the ground. He wrapped his hands around Hayden's neck, choking him and wrestling to get on top. Luciano punched him in the face – multiple times. Hayden was subjected to all of Luciano's pent-up anger. They exchanged a few more hits, received bruises, and spilled droplets of blood before finally getting separated by Nero and security guards.

"Get them out of here!" Nero ordered the security guards as they restrained Banion's men.

"They are not going anywhere." Luciano got up from the ground, wiping the dirt on his hands onto his trousers.

"No, you are not going anywhere. Don't you realize what you just did?" Nero obstructed the path, stopping Luciano from walking past him. Then he cut his scathing gaze to Paolo and Orfeo. "When did you two plan on stopping him? After he stabbed them to death in broad daylight?"

"That's enough, Nero," Luciano said with a frown.

While Nero continued his scolding, Luciano turned his head sideways, checking if the FBI agents were still there. One of them was gone.

Upon returning home, Luciano went in search of his wife for no other reason than simply wanting to be in her presence.

"What are you doing?" he asked as he entered the library.

His voice brought a stop to Nina's staring at the fireplace. She parted her lips to give a reply but Luciano's roughed up appearance had her speaking with her eyes instead. She looked as if she expected him to come back looking the way he did. He watched her stand up, and head his way until they met in the middle.

"What have you done?" Her eyes trailed over the small cuts on his cheek toward the dirt on his clothes. "Your hands." There was blood on them. She took his hands in hers, lines of concern written on her face.

"What are you thinking?" the timbre of his voice had Nina's heart beating faster.

He took a single step closer.

"Why?" she asked and took one back.

"Just tell me." He took another one forward.

"Right now?" She took one backward.

"Yes," his tone firm.

It was as if they were dancing. Although, Nina was forced to stop as she softly bumped into the leather chaise lounge.

"I wish you weren't so impulsive," she replied, her brows frowning ever so slightly.

The comment furnished Luciano's face with a lazy smile. As fast as it came, it left. His eyes dropped to the warm colour of her eyes. Intentional or not, she always managed to captivate him. Her eyes were cast at his own, it felt as if she was looking right through him. It didn't sit right with Luciano and so, he captured her supple lips.

"Why would you wish for something like that?" he inquired.

Nina's cheeks bloomed into a baby pink when he, with more force than he had to, pulled her closer by the waist.

"I don't have to tell you what you already know," she said.

"I don't know what you mean." He kissed her again. Hard. This time his hands were cupping her face. Only once she released a moan, he stopped.

"You do know or you simply don't allow yourself to admit it." She gave him a sugar-sweet smile. "That's what I think."

It had been a while since he last saw her signature smile be directed at him. It ignited a spark. He wanted Nina to lay bare before him. See how her sensitive skin reacted to his fingers brushing over it. How she would meet gaze his gaze head strong. How she would feel against him.

And that's what he did.

Before Nina could react, she laid on the chaise lounge. Her dress had ridden up her legs. The teasing of her black lingerie had Luciano sending her a burning gaze. Her bare skin shivered in anticipation as his hands roamed over the edge of it. Intoxicating; just like their all-consuming kiss that left Nina breathless. Although she wanted more.

Nina slipped out of his grip and got up. "Can you turn around?"

Luciano faced the fireplace as per her request. Just when he didn't think his heart could go any faster, it did. The zipping sound stopped and was followed by the creaking of leather. He didn't wait until she told him he could look again. He didn't have the patience.

"Do you still wish for me not to be impulsive?" Slate-grey eyes lingered on the tiny beauty marks on her olive skin.

She narrowed her eyes at him, her lips tipping up. "That's sly."

"It's just an honest question."

Luciano dropped his belt on the floor. Thump. That alone created a warm feeling to pool in Nina's stomach.

Jewellery was taken off her body, one by one until she reached for the clasp of her dainty necklace.

"No, keep it on," he said, moving closer as if he was a lion on the prowl. "I want it to be the only piece on you."

The shimmer of necklace's crystal was hidden behind the one on Nina's hand. "What about this one?"

"Want to get cute now?" Luciano said while the chaise lounge dipped under his weight.

The sweet smile she supplied him with morphed into a gasp as he grabbed her on either side to slide her closer to him. Light kisses turned into heavier ones, bruises being left behind at some places. At one point, he left Nina with a burning sensation after roughly taking off her undergarments.

"Touch yourself," he said in between his kisses.

The dusting of pink spreading from her cheeks all the way to her chest that heaved up and down at his order. Nina held eye contact with her husband, feeling thrilled and jittery as she gave him something to look at.

She bewitched him.

While Nina touched herself, he gave her breasts attention. He loved how responsive she was to his searing touch. It turned him on.

"How does it feel, Nina? Tell me."

"Good but-" she gasped since his tongue was caressing her nipples and began to moan.

"But?" He kissed the sweet spot on her neck.

"I'd rather have you."

Luciano glanced at his hands that were still as bloody as ever. How he longed to touch her there but hygiene stopped him from doing so. He wasn't the only one looking as his dirty hands though.

Nina added, "Not one of my brightest ideas."

He laughed and proposed, "Maybe another time? Something to look forward to."

She nodded with a smile. "We have till death do us part, right?"

"Yes, death. Another thing to look forward to."

Nina laughed along with him for taking her words out of context. Despite finding herself in unknown territory, he managed to make her feel at ease. Her worries about whether she was doing it right or looked good doing it washed away. Her laugh dwindled down to a radiant smile; she was just going enjoy their intimate moment. Nina traced the contours of his face with her other hand, feeling like he had taken her breath away.

"There is something else we can do," his deep voice pulled her back. "Though I can't promise you I'll be able to hold out for long."

"That's fine," she commented, wanting to rid him of the pressure to perform. "I just want you to come."

"What about yourself?"

"I think I'll be fine," she said softly, thinking how his voice alone could do the job.

As he positioned himself, Nina held her breath. She had been secretly yearning for this moment. Notes of sweat, sandalwood and freesia flowers hung in the air, the scents intertwined with each other, just like them. She felt herself slowly stretching out as he penetrated her. With every movement, he stopped for a second for her body to adjust, the gesture made her heart swell.

The uncomfortable pain was the last thing on Nina's mind, all that raced through her head was how she imagined her eyes to be in the shapes of ruby hearts.

"God, you're so handsome," her voice was a tiny whisper and sounded like she was almost out of breath.

"I'm trying to go slow, Nina," Luciano groaned before kissing her silky lips. "You're not making it easier."

"I'm sorry," she said despite not looking the part after kissing him back. "You can move now."

"Yes?"

"Yes."

Nina nuzzled her face in the crook of his neck, her sight turning black while feeling all of him inside her. Once she felt his hand gripping her hip, his movement became steadier. She listened to his breaths, his groans and his curses. The gentle approach from a few seconds ago seemed to have dissipated into thin air; it was rough and aggressive.

She was on cloud nine.

All of Luciano's focus was on his wife. In his eyes, she was divine and irresistible. He could go all day long if she wanted to. The exact moment he heard her moaning his name, he came inside her along with a similar sound coming out of his mouth.

He lay down on top of her, needing to rest for a minute. "Did you come?"

She hummed a yes. "It felt nice."

Luciano raised himself, his gaze resting on different parts of her, the afterglow making him smile for some reason.

"It did," he murmured in agreement.

The following day, Luciano received an unpleasant call. The second he heard his burner phone, foreboding thoughts festered in his mind. He had a hunch he would get an earful from a certain FBI agent.

"You were supposed to stay low!" Enrique García sounded like his teeth were gritted.

"The Bureau got wind of it, I suppose," Luciano said.

Enrique laughed in disbelief. "As if you don't already know. I already have my hands full and then you do this shit."

Luciano leaned back in his office chair. "You don't plan on making yourself useful?"

"I will for the right price."

"We already gave you your pay check." A harsh frown was etched onto his features.

"Yeah, well, bribing the judges isn't going to be cheap. They are going to want you behind bars. Someone has to pay for everything going on and, right now, that's you, buddy. They want the big fish – not some small-timer," Enrique said before sighing loudly. "I have to go now. My break is almost over."

"Enrique."

"Yes?"

"You can expect Nero to call you sometime this week."

"I like the sound of that."

27

CHAPTER 27

A thin layer of snow covered the streets of Lincoln Park, on the sides were piles of shovelled snow, and the scenery wasn't going to change anytime soon as big snowflakes fell from the grey sky. Parked cars had a thick blanket of snow on them, much like the streetlamps that emitted a warm orange glow. Winter wonderland at its best.

Frost-covered trees framed the red brick house of Affonso Gallucci, the underboss of The Outfit. Inside it, awaited welcoming embraces and a warm meal to share with the family.

"They are in a festive mood." Nina checked out the many Christmas lights brightening the outside of the house. "Is it your uncle's or your aunt's doing?"

"Both," Luciano said as he inserted the house key in the lock.

"I know you can but that doesn't mean that you should. Isn't it politer to knock or ring the bell?" She held him lightly by the arm.

He smiled as he swung the door open, and said, "No."

The roof above their heads was practically a second home to Luciano. This became apparent to Nina when she heard his aunt's voice, Rita, flow out of the living room, asking if it was indeed her nephew as she suspected. Before Luciano got the chance to respond, his uncle, Affonso, stuck his head out of the kitchen and confirmed his wife's suspicion out loud.

"I was just doing some tasting and I'm not one to toot my own horn but you'll be eating like horses tonight!" Affonso laughed.

"It's that good, huh?" Luciano said as he helped Nina take her coat off.

"Oh, you bet!" Affonso exclaimed.

Simply by going off looks, one could tell that Luciano and Affonso were related. However, unlike Luciano, Affonso had salt and pepper hair, a noticeable abnormality in his gait and an upbeat demeanour.

"It smells amazing. I already look forward to tasting it." Nina commented on Affonso's cooking and supplied him with a smile.

"You better be!" Affonso raised his brows and pointed a stern finger in the air. He walked over to them, with a limp, and embraced them. "I hope you two skipped lunch like I told you to."

After she was released by Affonso, Nina said, "It's completely empty." Nina rubbed her stomach with a soft laugh.

"You two look lovely!"

Nina turned her head at the female voice. It was Rita. She met with the woman's kind eyes and greeted her with a hug. Rita had a chin-length haircut, her ears were adorned with pearl earrings, and her fragrance was one that brought comfort.

Shortly after, they entered the decorated living room, bright red flowers of the Holy Night were sprinkled throughout the area, a lit-up tree sat in the corner, and Christmas carols played softly in the background.

Nina glanced at the Gallucci family. Smiling and unsmiling faces. Nicolò and Teodoro belonged to the former. Severino and his wife, Marietta, to the latter. Everyone was huddled at the sitting area, except for Marietta who seemed to have distanced herself from the rest and busied herself by setting the dinner table up. When her brother-in-law stood up with open arms, Nina had a sneaking feeling she was in for a treat.

"You're finally here!" Teodoro hugged Luciano tightly. "How could Christmas start without the family man?"

"Hello to you too," Luciano grumbled. "And stop saying that."

"It's a compliment," Teodoro retorted.

Luciano disliked Teodoro's comment. That much was clear to Nina, but she didn't know why it was inappropriate. It was a question she would have to ask her husband later on.

"Luciano, give me a hand will you?" Affonso called out before slinking back into the kitchen.

The same time Nina watched Luciano's broad back leave, she felt someone tug at her arm. She sent Nicolò a questioning gaze but he simply patted on the spot beside him. She smiled. It felt good to see him again. Speaking to one another in person was always better than doing it over the phone.

"How is everything going?" he asked as she sat down.

"Good, Nonno." Nina kept her answer short, aware of Teodoro and Severino listening in on the conversation.

Nicolò did a bob of the head. "That's good."

"That's all you're going to give us?" Teodoro spoke as a slow smile painted over the previous look of boredom. "No drama, gossip, no nothing?"

"Shut up," Severino said to Teodoro. "You always say this kind of shit."

Nina cut her aloof gaze to Severino, perplexity swimming underneath its surface. Severino's reaction seemed so unlike him. Then again, she didn't know the man. Her prejudices against him were taken into question.

"Teodoro, outside now," Nicolò's stern tone froze everyone in the sitting area.

"It was just a joke!" Teodoro's eyes widened.

"You and I are going to talk." Nicolò turned to Teodoro before exiting the living room. "Do you want me to drag you out of here?"

Before Teodoro got the chance to let out an insolent remark, he got quite literally dragged out of the room by his grandfather. The show got a smirk out of its spectators.

When Severino moved spots to sit beside Nina instead of across her, her posture became immensely rigid. Her mouth forgot how to smile and her wary eyes stayed on him.

"When you said things were good, I assume you were speaking about Luciano and you," Severino asked in a low voice to which Nina nodded. "Is it true?"

"Why would you want to know?"

The muscle along his jaw ticked. "I suppose I'm curious."

Nina's brain throbbed as she tried figuring out why he wanted to know. If he wanted to know about something this personal, he could've gone to Luciano rather than her. Their relationship was non-existent. What an odd situation to be in.

"It's true."

"How?" Severino's voice was laced in disbelief all the while having a look of genuine confusion on his facial features.

He did not get an answer as Marietta addressed them, telling them that dinner was ready. Nina rose from the couch but not before catching a glimpse of Severino. As expected, his usual mask of disgruntlement had slipped back on.

"Where are Nonno and Teodoro?" Affonso asked his son.

"Outside," Severino replied.

"Wait, I'll get them." Affonso placed the last steaming-hot dish on the table. "And don't start eating without us. I'm talking to you, Luciano!"

Nina sat beside her husband, suppressing a smile.

"I can see you trying to hide it," Luciano whispered to Nina.

"Of course you can."

Luciano briefly raised his eyebrows at her sarcasm. "You don't believe me?"

"I'm afraid I do," she whispered back, causing Luciano to hide his victorious smile behind his hand so the rest of the family wouldn't see.

Only now, Nina noticed his jewellery. Square cufflinks with a golden edge and black centre. The ones she had gifted him prior to their wedding. The ones she had already forgotten about. The gift she presumed to have been thrown in the trash can upon recipience.

"You're wearing them," she commented.

"Of course. It's my first gift from you."

"This night is full of surprises."

"Care to elaborate?" he asked.

"Later," she said before seeing the three men return and take up their seats at the table.

"You're always a handful," Rita said along with a chuckle and pinched Teodoro's cheek.

"I try my best," Teodoro replied back to his aunt.

Affonso cleared his throat in a loud manner, capturing everyone's attention. He extended his hands to Rita and Nicolò, who were on either side of him, and the rest of the family copied the action, creating a chained circle. They prayed before dinner.

Afterwards, everyone engaged in conversation which Nina had gotten used to now. It was just another difference between her and Luciano's family. She grew up with deadly silent dinners while he grew up with rowdy dinners.

Teodoro was the first one to dig his teeth into the food, stating how long he had been looking forward to this day. "It's even better than last year!" Teodoro said after taking a bite of dinner while kissing his aunt's cheek and raising his glass at his uncle.

"I try my best." Rita lifted her shoulder nonchalantly.

"We." Affonso eyed his wife, waiting for her to correct herself.

"We tried our best." She rolled her eyes along with a laugh.

Teodoro turned to Nina who sat across him. "It's true. It really is better." He took another bite. "God, I haven't eaten like this in eternity. Oh, no, wait I have. You can always go to their house for an excellent second-rate dinner." Teodoro cocked his head toward Severino and Marietta.

The comment caused Luciano to choke on his food and Nina to mentally drop her jaw since Teodoro wasn't exactly keeping the volume of his voice low. Nina was quick to hand her husband a glass of water while stroking his back.

"Are you okay?" Nina asked Luciano.

"Yes," Luciano said while keeping his hand in front of his mouth to kill his snickering.

"I'm done with this." Marietta dropped her cutlery on the plate and stormed out of the house.

When Teodoro made a whistling sound he received a glare from almost everyone at the table.

"You know you all want to agree," Teodoro said.

They did agree – in their head.

Rita was the first to stand up, announcing that she better go check on Marietta. She left but it didn't take long for her to come back without any success in bringing Marietta back to the table. She looked at Nina, her eyes pleading that she have a talk with Marietta instead.

"She's outside?" Nina asked Rita and got answered with a nod.

Why even consider sending Severino out to console Marietta? It's not like he's her husband or anything like that. The thought got Nina to sigh softly.

Ahead of her waited a talk that she wasn't looking forward to. Nina and Marietta simply didn't mesh well.

Nina grabbed her coat on the way before stepping outside the warm house. Thankfully, the snowfall wasn't as heavy as before. She laid her eyes on Marietta's hunched figure and gently draped the wool coat over her, startling her.

"Sorry for the surprise," Nina said after sitting on the freezing front doorsteps.

Marietta's red fingers traced the edges of Nina's coat. "Aren't you cold?"

"Not colder than you." Nina folded her arms to keep her body warmth from escaping. "Are you alright?"

"What do you think? You know what being an outsider is like." Marietta grumbled, "I'm sick of this. I swear to God, they think no one is worthy enough to carry their name."

"You know better than to truly believe that," Nina spoke gently with Luciano and Nicolò in the back of her mind.

"You're sticking up for them?" Marietta flung her an incredulous expression.

"For some, yes."

"You don't have to pretend here. I mean, I'd love to hear all about how well Luciano treats you but I think I'll pass." She then laughed to herself. "Maybe I should be happy to be married to Severino because at least it's not hell like yours – 'cause he's clearly already brainwashed you. God, I'm so done with this family."

Nina felt her body temperature go up as though it was the middle of summer. The insult about herself, she could let slide – she has had worse. The one about Luciano and her marriage, she couldn't ignore.

"You're in no position to talk to me like that." Nina narrowed her eyes at her. "Whatever problems and insecurities you have in your marriage, don't project them onto mine."

"What?" Marietta shot up, the coat slipping off and pooling on the ground. "I'm not projecting anything! You don't know what you're talking about!"

Nina also got up, wanting to be on eye level. "I'm not here to have a screaming match with you, Marietta."

Luciano's silhouette appeared in the doorway and Severino's loud footsteps sounded behind him. Unfortunately for Marietta, they heard her shouting.

"Did you just yell at my wife?" Luciano said in such a harsh tone that Nina could imagine Marietta being beaten black and blue.

"It's because she-" Marietta began.

"Don't try and blame it on me, Marietta. You were out of line," Nina said coldly.

"Alright, back off." Severino intervened. "I'll deal with this myself," he said in a lower tone.

Nina and Luciano watched them walk away into the darkness of the night, barely being able to outline their figures. Teodoro's voice got them to rip their eyes off the fighting couple.

Nina took in her brother-in-law's facial expression. "You're enjoying this more than you should."

"What's Christmas without a little drama?" Teodoro replied back.

28

CHAPTER 28

Drama was synonymous to fun and entertainment to Teodoro. He had a propensity to make impertinent comments, and Luciano was no stranger to it. The family man. That's what they called Luciano Gallucci – though only when he wasn't around to slap you for it. For a long time now, Luciano told his brother – and told him and told him – to not ever call him by that nickname again.

"I hoped to see a little more action from a fami-" Teodoro began but was quickly stifled by Luciano.

He got what was coming to him.

"You don't know when to stop, do you? You're a child with no manners," Luciano told his little brother before walking out of the freezing hallway and back into the living room.

The sight in front of Nina caused her anger from earlier to thin out. There wasn't enough room for both Nina and Luciano to be heated. She felt like one had to balance out the other.

"Follow me," Nina said to Teodoro after closing the front door and lead them to the kitchen's freezer.

She pressed an ice cube against his hurting cheek, her keen eyes unable to look away from his unusual silence. Normally, he would have already gotten a cheeky remark out by now. Nina regarded him as his blank face drowned in incomprehension.

"Why do you keep calling him that?" she asked as she lifted the small cube off his face.

"It's a fucking compliment," he grumbled.

"From my point of view, it looks like a pretty fucking unwanted compliment."

The harsh tone in which Nina spoke in had Teodoro stunned. It took a few seconds before he blinked again. He then mumbled, "Sweet Jesus." Teodoro snatched the melting cube out of Nina's hand and flicked it into the sink, all the while throwing her an ugly glare. "What do you even know? Goddamn nosy."

Nosy? That's rich coming from you.

"Nothing. I know absolutely nothing," she began, her voice wavering and her teeth were gritted. "But even then, I'm capable of telling that Luciano despises it when you call him that."

"What's going on?" Severino stepped into the kitchen.

How long has he been here? I didn't even hear him come back inside and Marietta is not with him either.

"Nothing special," Teodoro said to his older cousin. "Where's the wife?"

"She went home," Severino answered as his eyes kept darting between Nina and Teodoro. The red mark on his cousin's face drawing his attention.

"Why? Does she not like us?" Teodoro laughed quietly to himself. "Ah, well, the feeling is mutual."

Severino glowered at Teodoro. "I'm not going to force her to stay somewhere she doesn't want to be."

"Look at you! Husband of the year. Your attempt in saving your marriage is by letting her go?"

Such abysmal lack of respect seemed to be the final drop for Severino. Gone was the deep frown, a slow smile taking its place. An image unfitting of him in Nina's opinion but it accomplished what it was supposed to do as even Teodoro went silent.

"You do know when to shut up. Who hit you?"

Teodoro looked away, not wanting to admit it was his own brother.

Severino continued, "Do you mind speaking for him, Nina?"

"I'm not sure if I saw who did it," she said, her gaze as aloof as Severino.

"It wasn't Nina. It was Luciano," Teodoro grumbled.

Severino nodded. That was all he needed to hear to be in the loop of things. He set his eyes on Nina and no longer wore the smile on his lips. "Can I have a word with you in private?"

She narrowed her eyes and tilted her head ever so slightly but still told him that he could and followed him outside. The door was somewhat left ajar by Nina, and she kept a fair amount of distance between them.

"He's a little shit." He eyed Nina, not changing the angle of head causing it to look like he looked down on her. "He can be good if he wants to, but don't tell him I said that."

The last part got Nina to smile internally. Her reticence ensued, waiting for Severino to mention his wife – more specifically, the conversation she had with her.

"Did Marietta say anything that I should know of?" Severino stepped closer, his shadow now looming over Nina.

"Whatever she said or didn't say is hers to tell. Not mine, Severino."

His eyes sneered at her. "I hate it when people do that." He moved to lean against the cold railing. "But I can respect it."

"Can I ask you something?"

"Yes, but that doesn't mean I'll give you an answer," he drawled.

"Why did Luciano hit Teodoro?"

"Do you know what set this war in motion?"

She frowned at the question. "No."

And thus, Severino told her about the clash from four years ago. How Luciano and Teodoro lost their parents to an ambush from The Irish Mob, and how Luciano got his revenge that very same night by murdering the shooter and his family – irregardless of their innocence.

When Luciano informed The Family of his actions, he spoke in the voice of a stranger as if that night hadn't happened to him, but to somebody else. More so than others, he was painstakingly aware of how much he had fallen from grace. And while Teodoro openly revered his brother for his cold-blooded executions, others in The Outfit expressed their sharp disapproval since the young man's actions brought too much heat to them and bringing innocents into their world was unforgivable.

"They were right to rebuke Luciano. Some still do," Severino commented. "I'll be joining the others now if you don't mind."

Once he left, Nina took in a deep breath as she let it all sink in. No wonder he-. I have no words. Just as she saw Severino slink out of the hallway, Luciano entered it. The former whispered something, and it didn't take a genius to figure out what was said between the two. The solemn expression on Luciano faded into a phantom of a smile causing Nina's heavy heart to cry in his stead.

"There is somewhere I want to go."

Nina handed over his topcoat. "Now?"

"Yes."

The warmth of his hand seeped into her as he pulled her along. They got in the car and drove to a church that brought upon a wave of nostalgia onto Luciano. They stepped out of the vehicle yet didn't enter the house of prayer.

"Luciano?" Her eyes questioning him why they were there.

He had been called many things in his life but none carried the weight she brought along whenever she called him by his name.

"We used to come here on Christmas Eve. Every year. Back then, I didn't care much for it."

She wrapped her arm around his, her hand gently squeezing him. "You couldn't have known. You never know how limited your days are with the people you love."

"Despite the life we live?" The corners of his lips tipped upwards.

"It's only natural to hope for the best."

He shook his head. "I take what I can get."

"Is that how you see yourself?"

He didn't answer her, only giving her a weak smile. "How do you see me?"

Don't ask. Please. You know exactly how loaded your question is.

"More or less the same as yesterday."

"Oh, yes, Severino told you," his voice feigned as if his memory failed him. A rotten feeling burrowed inside Luciano. "There's nothing left to say about it."

"Then why do you sound as if you want to talk about it? Why did you ask me how I view you?"

"Why would I want to talk about it? I know what happened. I was there. If you think I haven't dealt with the loss of my parents then you're mistaken. I have." He went quiet for a while before speaking again. This time, notes of irritation tinged his voice, "What do you want from me, Nina?"

"I want you to stop avoiding my question. Why did you ask me how I see you?" She moved to stand in front of him, her hands on his chest and her warm eyes on his.

Underneath his mask resurfaced a deep-rooted feeling that he'd rather keep buried. "Answer me first," he managed to get out.

The reluctance bleeding through his voice was as clear as day to her. The weight of her opinion sat heavy on his shoulders. She understood that she wasn't meant to give him an answer to begin with but rather give reassurance that she wasn't judging him.

"I don't think any less of you, Luciano."

The words teetered at the edge of his tongue. It took a full minute before he said, "I'm ashamed of what I did." His shoulders sagged. "One of them was about Teodoro's age and the other, I don't know, about my age at the time." No longer did he need to mentally remove himself from this sin and confessing to it – outside a church no less – gave him the ability to move on from it. "It was anything but an eye for an eye."

Nina merely hummed in agreement before engulfing her arms around him. "And you won't do it again? Even when you go for their head?"

"It's a long time before that'll happen."

"How long?"

"Three months," he said with a finality to it.

"And then?"

"I don't know." Luciano inhaled her honey scented hair and kissed her on the forehead.

29

━ ◆ ━

CHAPTER 29

2⁰¹⁹ The tension within the walls of Luciano's office reached an all-time high.

Marietta was missing.

"She's not answering." Severino's fingers turned vermillion as he gripped his phone. At this point, his patience was as flimsy as a house of cards.

"Try again in a few minutes," Luciano said, keeping his refined composure.

"With all due respe-"

A third man entered the picture. Normally, Luciano told people off when entering his office without knocking but with his older cousin he could see it through the eyes.

Strolling inside the grim room was none other than Rodolfo Gallucci. One of the more, if not the most, competent captain in The Outfit and with a large following, it made him a force to be reckoned with. If they wanted to get Marietta, they needed him.

Severino didn't do anything to hide his disdain for Rodolfo. He couldn't stand him on a personal level, their personalities were simply too similar.

"Don. Severino." Rodolfo greeted them. "What's so urgent that you couldn't tell me on the phone?" He sat down and took out a flask.

Severino smacked it out of Rodolfo's tattooed hand. "Don't drink on the job when you're a lightweight. Marietta is missing."

Rodolfo stood up and got up in Severino's face. "Oh, really? Then tone down the attitude and I might actually consider lending you a hand."

Luciano raised himself to his full length, walked around his desk and separated the two headstrong men, the steely look in his eyes serving as a warning. Sometimes Luciano wished his grandfather was still the Don. When he ruled, his captains didn't dare to even bicker in his presence when doing business.

In spite of Rodolfo's domineering nature, he was an exceedingly obedient man, but only because he worshipped the hierarchy set in place. And so, he backed off.

Severino turned his back to them, needing to regain his cool before sitting down on one of the leather chairs. "The Irish kidnapped her," he said to Rodolfo.

"I told you, that's not possible. We already took care of that problem," Luciano interjected.

"Clearly, not good enough. She told me she saw them in the neighbourhood the night before," Severino argued as he tried calling his wife again. Alas, no one picked up. "Nothing," he clipped.

"And her father..." Rodolfo snapped his fingers trying to think of his name and face. It was a lost cause and since he couldn't remember her father for the life of him, he deemed the man as insignificant. "Does he know?"

"Yes," Severino answered.

"And?" Rodolfo said.

"He didn't care."

Rodolfo rolled his eyes at his cousin. "I'm not asking if he cares. I'm asking what he knows."

"He doesn't know anything. The man barely stays in contact with Marietta anyway," Luciano answered in Severino's stead. He sensed how much Rodolfo's condescending tone grated on Severino's nerves and didn't want their bad blood to take a physical form. "When did you last see her, Severino?"

"In the morning. She went on a morning walk."

"Rodolfo, I want you and your men in the neighbourhood. Look and ask around if there they saw anything suspicious – as nicely as possible." When he saw Rodolfo prematurely standing up, he added, "Just so you know everything we planned for tomorrow still stands."

"Will do, Don," Rodolfo said before picking up his flask and left.

"Protecting her was the one duty I was supposed fulfil," Severino said as chagrin writ on his facial features. "I'm going."

As soon as Luciano was left by himself, he dropped his head, his gaze the floor. Could it get any worse? He covered his eyes with his hand, the grip on his temples getting stronger by the second.

"Nina." Almost instinctively, her name flowed out of his mouth. She was alright, wasn't she?

Once again, Luciano went in search of his wife. He yelled out her name but was met with silence. He continued making his way through the hallways of the mansion and kept shouting, "Nina!" Finally, he checked the sunroom. She wasn't there either. He was feeling his heart in his throat now.

When he called her up, her ringtone rang throughout the sunroom. "Fucking hell, Nina." So, he called Bartolomeo as he went outside.

"Yes, Don?" Bartolomeo opened the call with.

"Where is Nina?"

"With me. We're gardening."

Even though he now knew she was safe, it wasn't until he saw it for himself that a shot of relief went through him. Luciano signed for Bartolomeo to leave them alone and bridged the distance between himself and his wife.

Unclouded amber eyes stared back at him. A sight he could be entrapped in forever. Golden hour was only the cherry on the top as her skin appeared ethereal. Her presence alone caused him to be no longer bereft of oxygen.

"I was looking for you," he spoke up.

"I can tell." She didn't go in detail just how distressed he looked and only said, "Something is bothering you."

"I thought you were my wife not a psychic?"

"They don't have to be mutually exclusive." She didn't want him changing topics and went back on track. "Is it because of tomorrow?"

"No," he sighed out heavily.

"What is it then?"

"Nothing you have to worry about." He studiously avoided her gaze, preferring to look at the effects of spring on the budding flowers. "Do you know how to shoot a gun?"

For wives of made men to be kept in the dark was anything but uncommon. At least, that was what she'd witnessed all her life. Exceptions were rare. Up until now, Luciano had thrown those preconceived notions into blazing flames. He had been very open and honest whenever she had questions. So his secrecy troubled her. And then that question of his. How strange, she thought.

"Yes, I know. But why?"

"You do?" He raised a single black eyebrow.

"Yes, and I wish you didn't look that surprised." Nina lightly pushed him by the arm. She elaborated, "Arturo taught me. Not that it mattered because I wasn't allowed a gun."

"Carlos?"

She shook her head, a bitter smile furnishing her visage. "You'd think so, wouldn't you? No, it was my uncle who didn't want it."

He hummed. "But it's good that you know."

"That doesn't mean I'm good at it. I never put it in practice."

"Really? I would've thought differently since you have plenty dirt on your hands by the looks of it." His eyes trailed to the dirt on her hands from all the gardening she had done.

He teased a smile out of her to which he could only respond by placing a singeing kiss on her lips.

"I didn't know I had a comedian for a husband," she mumbled against his lips. "I won't push for it but don't sell me pretty lies. There is something going on so don't tell me it's nothing. Just tell me that you can't tell me or don't want to tell me."

"Alright." He caressed her cheek.

You'd tell me if you couldn't tell me so that leaves the other. You don't want to tell me. It might concern my safety. No, he'd tell me if it did. It probably doesn't concern my safety or at least not directly, Nina thought to herself as she leaned into his warm touch.

Nina's silk robe hugged her figure as she exited the bathroom. Her steps led her to the vanity mirror before lowering herself to sit in front of it. From her peripheral vision, she could see Luciano coming closer until she felt his warmth radiating at her back. The hairbrush was taken from her slim fingers causing her to look at his reflection.

She quietly watched him brush her velvety dark brown hair. A sense of calm draped upon her features. To be cared for in such a gentle manner made her heart flutter. His eyebrows were drawn together and his mouth in a taut line. The contrast got her to release a breathless giggle.

He put a halt to his movement at the sound coming out of her and arched an eyebrow at her.

"Sorry. You can continue. I'll be as quiet as a mouse." Nina gave him a sweet smile.

He repeated the caring act once more, keeping the same serious expression on his face. He looked a bit daunting if Nina was being honest with herself yet at the same time thinking that she'd never tire of looking at him. When he got rid of the brush and felt his large hands on her shoulders, questions popped into her head. Just from the way his touch reached her, she could tell he was about tell her something of importance.

"Don't be cross with me. I didn't want to stir any unnecessary panic in you and I also hoped this situation would've been resolved by now but Severino's wife is missing," he revealed to which her lips parted in shock. "The Irish have her."

"What? Why? Did they demand ransom money?"

"No, they didn't. I have no idea why."

"You don't think they somehow know about tomorrow, do you? Oh God, Marietta." She placed her hands on top of her chest.

"We'll find her." Luciano increased the pressure he used on her shoulders before saying, "I want you to be near Bartolomeo tomorrow. At all times. Do I make myself clear?"

The look in his eyes caused ice to spread through her spinal cord. "Yes."

"Good." He lifted his hand off her shoulder, his fingers now stroking the side of her neck. "You always listen so well."

Light pink suffused her cheeks as she heard the low rumble of his voice. She grasped the tips of his fingers before asking, "Will you promise me to not to get hurt?"

"That's an unreasonable request."

"It's not unreasonable for me to want that." She mumbled, "Unrealistic maybe."

"I'll promise to be more careful."

"Be careful or be more careful than you usually are?" She arched a brow.

The corner of his lip went up. "We could write up a contract if you love the little details that much."

"I'd love that very much." She flashed him a genuine smile.

CHAPTER 30

The day for the Italians to make their move had come. They were in the early hours of Saint Patrick's Day and Luciano was dead set on recreating the path to hell in the city's underworld. Those who crossed paths with him were considered unfortunate.

"I don't think you should go," Nina said, her troubled eyes following Luciano's every move as he filled his gun with bullets.

"You're not changing my mind," he spoke in a monotone. Luciano slid his gaze to his wife. "Have you already forgotten what they did during your uncle's funeral?"

There was this cold yet calculating quality to him which was more unnerving to Nina than his usual display of rage. Him having bloodshot eyes didn't help either. The moment he roughly took hold of her face, she realized any other attempt to try and stop him was futile. Determination seeped out of his being.

Right then and there, she had a premonition she would lose a part of herself today.

"Or do you remember things differently than I do, Nina? Because I'm fairly certain you were there as well when they opened fire."

"My gut is telling me that this is a bad idea." She rested her hands on his forearms.

The faintest of smiles arose on his features. "Teodoro once told me we were a match made in hell. I'll have to tell him he was mistaken." The undeliberate smile was quick to fade into obscurity.

When he dipped his head, so their lips brushed, Nina already knew what was coming – and also realized it wasn't going to be anything gentle like last night. Her cheeks had the colour of a rose blooming on them as he captured her yielding lips. He was more greedy than usual, and she didn't mind it one bit.

The sound of knocking diverted Luciano's attention to the person behind his office's door.

"What is it?" Luciano said in a displeased tone as he let go of his wife.

"You have visitors, Mr Gallucci," Serena informed after opening the door.

"They're early," Luciano mumbled to himself. "You can leave early today, Serena."

"Oh, no but I'm almost done," the old maid said.

Luciano gave her a tight-lipped smile. "It's alright. You can leave."

"Of course, Mr Gallucci," Serena said as she gulped before parting with a smile that was only returned by Nina.

Nina took the loaded gun off the large desk, her eyes lingering on it before handing it over to her husband.

"Let's not keep them waiting," she said as she suited up to be the elegant and sophisticated wife of their Don.

"Let's. But make no mention of Marietta. I want their focus on the task at hand. Besides, Severino and Paolo are already on it."

"I didn't plan to," she replied, grabbing the police uniforms off the armchair and followed the shadows of his steps.

"I forgot the-," Luciano was about to return to his office until he spotted the blue-coloured uniforms in Nina's arms.

"I got it."

Four men dressed like mafioso occupied the sitting area. One consigliere, two capos, and one soldier. Nero and Rodolfo were engaged in conversation, Orfeo was on the phone and Teodoro had thrown his head on the couch's headrest, looking bored with everything around him. Nina greeted all of the familiar faces with her signature smile. Serenity seemed to hang around everyone's heads; unlike Luciano who had dark clouds hanging above his.

"You won't mind if leave them here, right?" Nina said to Nero as she set the uniforms down beside him.

Nero moved to make more space, his hand reaching out to touch the fabric. "Of course not. They look convincing."

"Can someone enlighten me why you're all this early?" Luciano said.

"Better early than never!" Orfeo said with a belly laugh after putting his phone away.

Luciano eyed his uncle. The sheer stupidity and lack of ingenuity was an eyesore to him. For a capo, Orfeo made little to no money for The Family. On the contrary, he stood in red. In Luciano's younger years, he'd wonder why his uncle got the high-ranking position he did but eventually realized that Orfeo was family.

"Does anyone fancy a cup of coffee?" Nina asked the men.

Everyone except for Luciano seemed to care for one. Nina headed off to the kitchen where she stumbled upon her bodyguard, Bartolomeo, who was looking out the window.

"Why don't you join them?"

"I think I prefer your company, Boss."

"Coffee?" She plucked the cups out of the cabinet.

"No, thank you. I already had one. Even if I did want one, I'd make it myself. I am subservient to you."

The reminder of their positions got Nina to sigh softly. "I was being nice. Can you just take it?"

Bartolomeo pondered over it. "I might."

"You used to be the enforcer, right? Shouldn't you go with Luciano? He thinks highly of your skills, and it's not as if I'll be left without protection." She glanced at the guards walking the perimeter.

Bartolomeo shifted his weight to his other foot, clearing his throat in the process. "I was but my priorities have changed since."

"I see," she merely said while putting the hot cups on a serving tray.

She brought the coffee to the men and listened to them discussing their plan in great detail. Even her walk toward them was poised and proper, so much so that the hot liquid mimicked a calm sea. The ornate silver tray was placed on the small table and the cups of coffee were placed in front of the men by Nina.

"No, give it to me," Rodolfo said to Nina making her lift the cup off the table again and handing it directly over to him.

The tone Rodolfo used, drove Nina up the wall. It reminded her of her father. She couldn't stand him. Of course, her first impression of Rodolfo didn't help either as it was when he was absolutely besotted during her wedding reception.

"Here you go." Nina mustered up the sweetest smile she could.

Lastly, she gave her husband a cup despite him telling her he didn't want any. It was obvious he didn't sleep a wink.

"Thank you." His gaze briefly softening when they locked eyes.

"You're welcome."

"Did you hear what happened to Marietta, Nina? You should be careful." Teodoro then asked to no one in particular, "Is there any news on her by the way?"

"I thought Paolo and Severino were still looking," Orfeo mumbled against the edge of his cup. "Ah, shit!" He burned his tongue.

"No. No leads," Rodolfo answered Teodoro.

Nina slinked away, heading back to the kitchen as she dwelled on her last conversation with Marietta. If Luciano hadn't told her Marietta had been kidnapped by Banion's men, her line of thought would've brought her somewhere else. That she had run away. Or that Severino had snuffed her flame out. Then again, The Irish were known to drag innocents into their wars – like they recently did in New Orleans and Chicago. Or the opposite was true, and Marietta had gone to them to rat on the Gallucci family in order to be freed from their clutches. All scenarios struck Nina as probable. Granted, not all of them were equals.

"What do you think happened to Marietta?" she asked in a somewhat sotto voce to Bartolomeo.

His non-existent brows frowned at the question. "Did Luciano not tell you? She's-"

"No, he did tell me."

"Am I missing something?"

"No, maybe I'm looking too much into it," Nina said more to herself than Bartolomeo.

"Boss?"

"It's only that-"

Just then Luciano entered the space, prompting Nina to stop talking and turn around. He donned the uniform of a policeman.

Her lashes fluttered as she took in his appearance. He wore it well. Really well.

"I'm going," Luciano said to Nina and kissed her goodbye. It was just another day at work.

"I'll see you later," she forced out of her mouth before he left her side.

She brought the serving tray in front of her chest, hugging the cold item as she stared at the closing door. Tempted to beg him not to leave. She moved to the window, watching the made men dressed as policemen walk to their cars.

"Quite the view, isn't it?" she remarked as she regarded them.

"Certainly."

"Bartolomeo?"

"Yes, Boss?"

"Would you think badly of me if I put you in a difficult position?"

The imposter policemen were face to face with the wide-open doors of a remote church. Every year on this day and at this time, the head of The Irish Mob, Cillian Banion, visited this place with his family before going out to celebrate Saint Patrick's Day.

The execution of a murder mattered a great deal in their circles. Where, how and who you killed send out a signal to others. There were a few places that were considered off-limits when it came to warfare in the eyes of a mobster.

Just like Cillian had crossed that line, Luciano would too.

While Luciano wouldn't be the first mafioso to spill a rusty red colour inside a church, he would be the first to do it in a grandiose manner.

"It's our time to shine." Orfeo clapped Nero on his lower back.

Nero and Orfeo were up to the task of escorting the civilians out of the church since they didn't want any collateral damage. Their uniforms, of course, helped prevent an escalated form of panic and chaos.

"I'm still not convinced I should be the one leading this," Nero mumbled under his breath.

"You have a trustworthy face," Luciano said to Nero.

"Comparatively speaking," Teodoro quipped as he adjusted his grip on the green jerrycans.

Luciano and the others honed in on Cillian Banion. Something was off. Luciano's eyes swept over the pale faces of the civilians as they exited the body of the church, but Cillian's wife and son weren't amongst them.

"Get up, Banion! And put your hands in the air," Luciano shouted at him.

Cillian Banion obediently did as he was told, not showing any signs of fright.

"They're not here," Nero said in a low voice to Luciano.

"I know. Get Orfeo and keep going, make sure the civilians leave and don't linger around. I don't want any eyes."

"Alright."

Once silence ensued in the church, Luciano heard the closing of the front entrance. It was Nero letting him know that they had done their part.

Unease nestled into Luciano's heart as Cillian looked him dead in the eyes. Something was wrong.

"You filthy rats!" Cillian shouted from the top of his lungs – as the head of the Irish Mob – and seven of his men stormed the building through the backdoor.

Quickly, Teodoro and Rodolfo aimed their guns at the Irish soldiers while Luciano kept his on their leader. Luciano locked his jaw, hard enough that it felt like his teeth were breaking. This was bad. Even if Nero and Orfeo somehow knew to return, they'd still be outnumbered.

"Jesus, Mary, and Joseph! I get to meet Don Luciano in the flesh," Cillian spoke in a high-pitched tone to mimic a fan meeting their celebrity crush. "You don't dress like one though."

"Careful there. By the time your men pull the trigger on me, my bullet is already between your eyes. You can be sure as hell that I'll take you down with me," Luciano said, his voice laced in cold fury.

From his peripheral vision, Luciano could see a slow smile creeping up Teodoro's face while Rodolfo soundlessly recited a prayer.

"I'm too frail and old. I'm not one for change and...you, your father, and his father have overstayed your welcome. I told you I'd clean up my city," Cillian said as the veins in his forehead became more and more visible with each second.

In this life, when one puts bullets in someone else, they should be ready to take it as well. Luciano agreed with that line of thinking ever since he took the oath.

In this life, when one puts bullets in someone else, they should be ready to take it as well. Luciano agreed with that line of thinking ever since he took the oath, but this time he didn't. He didn't want death to push him into the depths of hell; not yet. For some reason, his mind drifted to Nina; to her plea that whispered into his ears. He internally sighed. Anything to hear her angelic voice as he awaited his inevitable death.

31

CHAPTER 31

"This is madness, Boss." Bartolomeo floored the gas pedal.

Nina gripped the gun in her hand as if it was a lifeline. As they raced toward the church Luciano said he'd be at, her hands became clammy but her fixation on reaching her husband grew. She couldn't stay put, couldn't wait until his bleeding body returned to her. Behind her impassive facial feature, hid great trepidation.

"I'm well aware."

Her bodyguard let out a breathless laugh.

"If this won't kill me then I'm sure Luciano will end my life for bringing you in grave danger."

"It was on my orders," Nina said.

"Not to be disrespectful but I don't think that will make a difference."

"My husband is a just man."

"True but do you think he'll be just when it comes to his wife. I've been an observer for most of my life and from what I've seen, Luciano has grown...how to say it? He has grown accustomed to your presence."

If it wasn't for the situation they were in, Nina would have chuckled at his wording. Then she spotted Nero jogging away from his car and Orfeo who walked with the legs of a newborn foal.

"Pull over! It's them."

Nina immediately felt Nero's vigilant eyes on her and Bartolomeo. His speed to faltered immediately. She steeled herself when she saw Nero shaking his head as if he couldn't believe what he was seeing. He would no doubt try to stop her.

"What are you doing here?" exasperation filling Nero's voice.

"Getting Luciano out of that damned place." Nina nodded her head at the church.

"I don't have the fucking patience for this," he whisper-yelled at her. "What's wrong with you?" Nero narrowed his eyes at Bartolomeo.

"Calm down. We have time. Shots haven't been fired yet," Orfeo said to Nero.

"That's the problem you fuckin' idiot!" Nero said to his uncle Orfeo. "You" – he pointed at Nina – "back in the car. Bartolomeo come with me."

"I don't take orders from you," Bartolomeo said.

Nero laughed bitterly and said, "Forgive me, Nina, but bullet in the leg is better than one in your lungs or stomach."

The second Nina saw Nero point his gun at her leg, she pointed hers at Orfeo's head.

"It's tit for tat." Nina let out a harsh breath. "This is ridiculous! I'm a better shot than him." She redirected their focus on Orfeo's poor attempt to hide his excessive trembling.

Nero's jaw became a hard set. "You're pointing a gun at a Made Man. You may be my cousin's wi-"

"I don't remember ever taking an oath that bound me by the same rules as you. The only oath I've taken is the one that involves my husband," Nina's tone was steely.

A dangerous smile grew on Nero as he lowered his gun and looked at his watch. "If not before then he definitely should be out by now. We're going in." He began stepping away. "Don't just stand there, Orfeo. Grow some balls for God's sake because Nina has more than you." Nero ran toward the awfully quiet church and Orfeo copied his actions.

Thank you? Nina thought to herself.

"What do you want to do, Boss?"

"Let's look for another entrance," Nina said.

Alarm bells went off at the sight of an already opened back door. Bartolomeo signed for them to be even more stealthy before peeking inside whilst slowly pushing the door open. Nina slipped inside, keeping careful watch of any dangers. Her eardrums felt like they could tear at the sound of her heartbeat, so loud and so fast. The further they moved into the dark corridor, the clearer they heard a menacing yet boisterous male voice of an older man.

Who? Nobody I know.

"Even more visitors! Blondie and...you. I didn't know so many people wanted me dead." The man laughed.

Blondie? Shit. Nero.

They were close to rounding a corner but when Bartolomeo quickly moved back, Nina stilled. She looked at him with questioning eyes to which he pressed a single finger to his lips. Furtively, she took in the dreadful image Bartolomeo had seen. Luciano. There he was in the middle of the aisle, held at gunpoint by a man who missed one or two fingers.

No, the voice inside her head quivered.

"Anyway, it's time we clean up this infestation but before that happens, I think you owe my boy an apology, Luciano. You haven't been uh, very nice to someone here. Now this is what I call sweet, sweet revenge, Dean," the man continued speaking.

Listening to them caused an ugly feeling to burrow inside her stomach. Sensing what Dean was about to do, she raised her gun in the shadows and aimed with precision for Dean's head.

"Where do you want it?" Dean taunted Luciano. "Or maybe I should skin you alive? How would you like that!"

Over my dead body.

She shot Dean in the head. Right above his ear to be exact.

Panic and chaos broke out. For the briefest of moments, Nina made eye contact with Luciano, his face losing all colour when he was able to make her out in the shadows. She heard another gun go off. Bartolomeo's large hand grabbed her by the arm and pulled her out of the way at breakneck speed.

Holy fuck.

"Stay low," he said as he fired at the Irish men.

Six more Irish men left.

By now, Luciano and the others had moved spots. Nina prayed the pews would hold up and protect them against the bullets. She assessed the situation and a funny thing happened. While all Irish soldiers risked their lives to protect their boss, one of them tried escaping. Not wanting to leave anything up to chance, Nina aimed her gun and shot him in the back resulting in his limp body to fall over.

That same time another person fell to the ground. It was Teodoro.

"I'm calling a truce!" Cillian yelled when he was the only one left standing – not counting the dead and severely wounded.

"Drop the gun and then we'll talk about a truce," Luciano responded.

Nina was glued with her back to the wall. Her eyes focused on the blood dripping down Bartolomeo's arm and her ears focused on Luciano, he sounded out of breath.

"Fine," Cillian clipped.

The gun hit the floor with a loud thud allowing Nina to breathe a little better. She put her gun away, helped Bartolomeo get out of his suit jacket and used it to put pressure on his wound.

"Before we end this, tell me where she is," Luciano demanded.

"You have me lost here, Son," Cillian said.

"Call me that again, Banion, and you're dead. Marietta Gallucci. Where is she?"

"Hand to God, I have never heard of this woman. You are looking in the wrong place. Let me leave and I'll prove it. You have my word." Cillian held his right hand on top of his heart.

A small smile played on Luciano's lips. "I believe you," he said rather abruptly; he was never really sold on the idea of Marietta having been kidnapped by Cillian.

Then, Luciano shot at Cillian Banion. The first piece of lead went through his foot, the second one went in his stomach and the third in his throat because Luciano wanted to hear him choke on his own blood. He got his revenge. For what they did four years ago, for their hit attempt in New Orleans and for the spilt blood of his family in Chicago.

"Go on, Boss," Bartolomeo told Nina as he nudged her hand off his now-wet jacket.

She showed him a tiny smile, her eyes slightly teary and squeezed his good arm. Not only had he backed her up when most wouldn't, he'd also saved her life.

"Thank you for everything," she said to which he responded with an awkward smile.

"Nina!" Luciano strained voice rang throughout the small church.

His booming voice should be anything but comforting yet Nina welcomed it with open arms. The tension in her body returned when she saw all of him. He had been shot in the leg. When he stood right in front of her, he wrapped his arms around her.

"You have no idea how much trouble you're in; and you only have yourself to thank for that because I wouldn't be alive if it wasn't for you."

"Luciano, you're bleeding. You need to stop the bleeding." She tried pushing him off her.

"I'll be fine."

"He's losing consciousness! Teodoro's starting to lose conscious-ness!" Nero shouted, getting everyone's attention.

Dread blanketed over everyone.

"Bring him to my car, Nero," Bartolomeo sprang into action.

"Go with him, Nina. You know what to do. Take care of him for me," Luciano said to her, the strain clinging onto his voice worsening.

"I will."

32

CHAPTER 32

After Nina and Bartolomeo left with Teodoro, Luciano took a moment to pull himself together. The job wasn't done yet. He barked out orders to the three men to take care of the bullet-riddled bodies while he would take care of the bloody church.

"Rodolfo, call some of your men to start digging." Luciano looked at the massacre. "It'll take a while to finish this up."

"I'm on it, Don."

Luciano picked up one of the jerrycans that Teodoro left outside the church and let the gasoline spill out. A burning church would cause enough of a distraction while they were busy giving Cillian Banion and his men their very own graveyard. After dousing the building, and after all corpses were taken out, Luciano let flames consume the house of prayer.

What a sight it was.

"It's better if you go and get that taken care of." Nero nodded at Luciano's bleeding upper thigh. "Think you can drive on your own?"

Luciano scowled. "No, you're right. Oh, and Nero, don't answer any of García's calls. I need to figure out some things before I'll talk to him."

Nero inclined his head. "Could you call me if there's news about Teodoro."

"I'll call if there's bad news."

"I might as well turn my phone off then."

Luciano was being stitched up by Dr Ricci. He leaned his head against the white wall and groaned when the needle pierced his skin. Next to him laid a small surgical tray. Its contents where chunks of the bullet that were coated with his blood. The tinier pieces of the bullet remained inside his leg.

"Congratulations on finishing medical school by the way," Luciano said to the young woman. Any kind of distraction sufficed.

"Thank you for the flowers you sent. They were lovely."

Luciano didn't remember ever sending her flowers. "Thank my wife for that."

"Oh, yes, I saw her come in with Teodoro."

"Who's working on my brother right now?"

"My mother," Dr Ricci said as she did the final stitch.

"Good." He grabbed the larger bullet pieces off the tray, stuffed them in his pocket and stood up. He said under his breath, "She knows what to do."

"I don't know if you already want to be moving arou-"

"Thank you for fixing me up, but I know my limits. If you don't mind, I'd like to pay my brother a visit." Before leaving, he looked over his shoulder. "For the record, I was never here and the same goes for my brother. Alright?"

"Alright." She smiled and gave him a compliant nod like her mother had taught her. Being family with people like him felt like a burden at times. Being family with people like him also meant her tuition fees for medical school were paid for. "Wait," it slipped out of her mouth before she realized it.

What now?

Luciano stopped before fully turning around. "Yes?"

"Where is Rodolfo? He told me he was going to your house this morning. He never tells me- and then you and your brother come in here looking like- I'm trying to say-" She looked as if she was going to cry. "What I'm trying to say is-"

"Take it easy. You aren't a widow, and your kid isn't fatherless. Alright?"

She pressed her lips together and simply nodded.

Ignoring the pain in his leg, Luciano hurried to the operating room. He made out Nina's hunched figure from down the hall. The red light above the closed doors were still on. His footsteps seemed to have alarmed her since she instantly looked up, her shoulders sagging when she saw it was him.

She got up. "There's no new news on Teodoro yet. How are you feeling?"

"I'm doing great," he drawled.

"Luciano," she began but froze when he gripped her by her upper arms.

"Don't use that tone on me, Nina. Do you have any idea what you did? The only thing keeping me sane right now is the knowledge that I don't have to hold your fucking funeral."

"Maybe your impulsive nature is rubbing off on me?" She gave him a weak smile.

He smiled widely at her. "Oh, really? So, this is my fault now?"

"What was I supposed to do then? What about me? Was I supposed to hold your funeral?"

Luciano briefly averted his gaze when he saw her indignant eyes well up. "Nina-"

"No, tell me," she said as tears silently streamed down her face. "I couldn't stand by like I did in New Orleans. I couldn't. When you left this morning, it felt like you were walking to your grave."

Luciano released his iron grip on her. How could he fight her when she wore her emotions on her sleeves like that? His movements may have been a bit rigid but he embraced her instead and kissed her on the temple. His hand smoothing over her hair, trying to soothe her. His other hand checked if she still had a gun on her body. She did.

"No, I'm angry with you." She made a poor attempt at trying to pry him off her.

"So am I, so deal with it."

From the corner of his eye, Luciano saw Bartolomeo walking up to them with drinks in his hands.

"Leave us," Luciano's tone rang cold as he watched the middle-aged bodyguard put the drinks down.

"Yes, Don." Bartolomeo looked at Nina and sent her a ghost of a smile. "Boss."

Luciano felt his wife's eyes burning through his skull. He guessed she didn't like the tone he used on her bodyguard.

"There are no excuses for what he did," he spoke.

"He saved my life." She crumpled the fabric of his white dress shirt in her fists.

"He didn't have to if he never brought you there in the first place."

"I would've gone your way whether he came with me or not. It's me – and only me – who should receive your anger. Not him."

Luciano closed his eyes and lowered his head on her shoulder. One day seemed to last ten years. He inhaled her scent; it was the same as his. Fear and blood hung around them like wasps.

She dirtied her hands for him.

She lost her innocence.

"We're not having this conversation right now," he mumbled. "You got the gun from my closet, I assume."

"Yes."

He moved past her and sat on a chair. When he wanted her to drop the pretence of being a saint, this wasn't it – far from it. He had driven her to sacrifice a part of herself.

"I thought you said you weren't good at shooting," he said.

"No, I said that knowing how to shoot a gun doesn't automatically mean you're good at it. I said that it didn't mean that I was good at it. I never said that I wasn't good at it. There is a difference." She sat beside him and had her palm facing up, waiting for him to share his warmth.

Luciano's gaze slid from her empty hand to her warm eyes. One moment she was easy to read, the other moment she wasn't. He needed her to yell at him. He needed her to lessen the guilt that was slowly creeping up his chest.

He reached out, intertwining their fingers.

She was supposed to be under my protection, the thought brought a low chuckle to the surface. I have to change my ways. I can't follow in Nonno's footsteps. Same goes for Dad – not that he was a widow for long.

"What is that look on your face?" she asked.

He ripped his eyes off the floor. You don't want to know what I'm thinking.

"I'm sorry you had to kill for me. I will never put you through that again," he solemnly said to his wife.

His body temperature went up after she rested her head on his tight shoulder. Reading her face was impossible now. Their reflection on the long window didn't help either. Brown locks of hair hid her features, and her gaze was cast down.

"I'd prefer it if you thanked me instead."

Thank you for killing for me? Thank you for saving me.

Luciano's lips were glued. He had trouble getting the words out. An apology was more appropriate in his mind.

The clock's long hand moved by five minutes.

"Thank you for everything."

"Thank you," she softly followed with.

Why she thanked him, Luciano didn't quite know. Guesses were thrown around in his head, but self-doubt shut most of them down. He let it go for now. Leaving it for another time to ponder over.

Nina lifted her head off his shoulder, took a deep breath and wet her lips. He handed her one of the drinks Bartolomeo had left behind.

She accepted it and took a big gulp of water. She noticed Luciano glancing at the red light. "Teodoro's strong-willed. I can't imagine him letting go. He's probably too curious to see what happened to Marietta."

She got a laugh out of him which made her smile in turn.

"That's true."

"They claimed they didn't have her." Nina referred to Banion's statement in the church. "Did you mean it when you said you believed him?"

"Yes, I did." He corrected himself by saying, "I do."

"You don't think she tipped The Irish off today?"

"I don't know. She could have if she wanted to be rid of us. What bothers me is that they knew we were coming. I suppose she could have used a middleman; it would explain Banion not knowing of Marietta's existence. This isn't looking good."

Especially for Severino.

Luciano let go of Nina's hand before dialling Severino's number.

"Where are you right now?" Luciano got straight to point the second Severino answered.

"At home. I'm going through her stuff. Maybe get a clue or something."

"Leave it. Marietta is with me. We're at the hospital. Come quickly."

"What? What happened?" Severino raised his voice then muttered, "So it really was Banion."

"Just hurry up. Bartolomeo is keeping watch outside, he'll tell you where to find us," Luciano said before ending the call.

The next person on Luciano's list was Bartolomeo.

"Yes, Don?" Bartolomeo opened the phone call with.

"If Severino comes up to you and asks about Marietta, send him our way. You won't utter as much as a word about what happened earlier today. Teodoro isn't here. Nina isn't here. Only Marietta and I are here. Do I make myself clear?"

"Marietta is with you?"

Luciano could hear the frown in his voice. "You know what lying is, right?"

"No, yes, I understand, Don. It's all clear."

"Good." Luciano hung up.

"It's a trap," Nina spoke up.

"It's only a trap if Severino is guilty of something."

"Do you think he'll show up?"

"I can only hope. If he doesn't, it means he knows I just lied to him. If he doesn't come, I'll have to assume the worst. That he is a rat – like his wife."

Nina sat on the edge of her chair. The more she thought about it, the greater her headache became. "But if Severino and Marietta were in this together, why did they say she was missing?"

"Kidnapped," Luciano corrected. "Maybe he was putting up an act?"

"Why would he do that?"

"Why? Originally, I didn't plan on bringing my uncle, Orfeo, with me." Luciano's voice became blank, "Severino was supposed to be there."

33

CHAPTER 33

The hospital lights appeared cold against Luciano's skin or maybe Nina's eyes were playing tricks on her. She took other sketches of him from her memory and compared him to a wilting flower. It was as if his skin was see-through paper, his bleary eyes brimmed with blood, and his posture had become that of a tarnished statue.

How could he not find himself in such a state when young flowers were being plucked off the family tree. The first flower went missing. The second one was close to dying. The fate of the third flower had yet to be decided.

Nina's fixed stare was on the doors Severino was supposed to walk through. She glanced at Luciano; uncertainty bled into his visage.

Affonso walked through the doors to which Nina had to hide her surprise. He headed in their direction with haste, although his limp didn't make it easy.

Why is he here? Nina thought. Did Severino call him?

"Follow my lead," Luciano said to her in a low voice.

"How is she?" Affonso asked them.

Luciano responded by simply pointing at the closed doors of the operating room.

A gloom fell over his expression, Affonso continued, "How bad is it?"

"We don't know yet," Nina said.

Affonso took a seat opposite of them. His hand massaging his limping leg. "That bastard doesn't know when to stop. He tried to get me all those years ago and now he goes after my only daughter-in-law. Bastard! You were able to get Cillian today, right?" His eyes flung to Luciano.

"Yes, he's gone," Luciano said.

Nina noted how Luciano tried to keep his lies at a minimal. Perhaps he wasn't used to lying to him. Perhaps he was worried his uncle could spot the lies of a boy he had known since birth.

The lies were a necessary evil. As Severino's father, Affonso might want to protect his son from Luciano by alerting him.

Nina supplied Affonso with a near-invisible smile when regarded her. She scolded herself inside her head for not looking flawless. Her expression was fine, but her hair and clothes were anything but.

He can't know I was at the church.

"It's awful, really. I came as soon as Luciano called me," she explained away her appearance. Affonso's slight frown was still in place, therefore she added, "It's Luciano's blood. He was shot in the leg."

"Really? No permanent damage I hope." Affonso blinked in shock.

"I was told not," Luciano said.

Footsteps sounded through the eerily quiet hallway. Severino joined them at last. Rather than seeing Luciano's reaction, Nina heard it. A deep sigh of relief slipped past his lips.

"Not yet," Luciano mumbled to Nina.

Not yet? What do you mean? Nina kept her thoughts to herself as she decided it was best to lock her lips shut.

"Where is she?" Severino asked, his eyes darting around.

"She's being operated on," Luciano replied, showing little to no emotion.

You're still testing him? Nina watched them, wanting to jump in. Cruel.

"What?" Severino clipped. "You somehow forgot to mention how bad it was when you called me?"

"I couldn't have you driving to the hospital in distress," Luciano explained to which his cousin scoffed. "You were right. It was Banion."

Severino sent him a scathing glare. He stepped closer to his Don causing the latter to tilt his head. "Is this your idea of an apology?"

Don't you think it's enough? He truly believes you. Nina's light touch on Luciano's arm conveyed her thoughts over to him.

Luciano sighed. "She isn't here."

"Luciano?" Affonso said while standing up.

"What do you mean?" Severino spoke at the same time as his father.

"Marietta was never here, Severino. I lied. I had to check whether you're a rat or not. For all I knew, you might have been working together with her-"

Severino interrupted Luciano by saying, "Stop right there. You thought I would sell out my own blood?! What's wrong with you?"

Affonso grabbed his son by the shoulder and pulled him back. It looked an awful lot like Severino was ready to give Luciano a black eye.

"If Marietta isn't here, where is she?" Affonso inquired his Don.

"I don't know to be frank," he began.

"You have to be fucking kidding me," Severino muttered.

Luciano continued, "But I might be able to give you a concrete answer after I make a call. Do you have a burner phone on you?"

"Of course, always." Affonso handed one to Luciano.

Luciano turned to Nina. "Could you tell them everything while I make this call?"

"What does everything entail?" she asked him.

"Everything from start to finish including my reasons for suspecting Severino."

"Okay," she said.

"Thank you, Nina."

That better be an important call you're making. Nina watched his back as he moved to get some privacy. Now that I think about it, I don't think I've ever seen mamma speak on such affairs. Clearly, our duties as wives don't always overlap.

Nina did what was asked of her. She started with her arrival at the church; what she heard and saw inside the church – leaving out what she did in it. Afterwards, she told them who was really in the operating room, prompting worry to flit across their eyes; and lastly, she presented them with an explanation why Luciano tested them.

She stayed silent as she watched them take it all in, especially Severino. She expected him to express his concerns for his wife in some form, but he didn't. It was unclear what was going on inside his head.

They might not have been on good terms with each other but even then... I suppose it's not unlikely that Marietta ran away. She saw her husband return to her side. That was pretty quick.

The last person on Luciano's list was Enrique García. An FBI agent who many saw as an odious man. He was the last person Luciano wanted to ask a favour from. The price he'd have to pay wouldn't be pretty.

"I have García looking for her," Luciano told everyone.

Hours upon hours passed by before the glaring red light went off. Like Dr Ricci told Luciano, her mother had indeed been the one saving Teodoro's life as she was the one exiting the room.

"The operation was successful. Teodoro's going to make it," Dr Ricci informed them. "You've got an exceptionally resilient brother, Luciano. We have to move him, but we'll have to be discreet, so it might be better if there isn't an entourage."

A chuckle came out of Luciano. He ran a hand through his black hair, he could breathe again.

The good news dispersed the grey clouds hanging above everyone's head.

Thank God. Oh, no, I think I'm going to cry. She rested her hands on top of her chest. No, keep it together, Nina.

"We're in your debt, Emma," Affonso said to Dr Ricci.

"Exactly, so let's get him quickly out of here before too many people catch wind of it," Dr Ricci said.

Just then the burner phone went off. Luciano's peace of mind flapped its wings.

"I have to take this. Nina, you go with her." He was reminded of her bloodied clothes when he looked in her direction. She wasn't exactly low-profile at the moment. "Never mind."

"I'll go," Affonso offered before following Dr Ricci's lead.

Luciano answered the call. Nina guessed it was García although she had no idea who he was.

Maybe one of those friends in high places.

She, along with Severino, listened in on Luciano's conversation.

"Not in Chicago?"

So, she did run away.

"She became what?" disbelief coloured Luciano's voice. He looked Severino in the eye and repeated García's words, "She became an informant."

Nina mouthed a 'no' while Severino seemed to have shut down.

Why hadn't I considered this an option? I didn't want to. The worst possible outcome so much so that her seeking help from The Irish was preferable. This can't be happening. This can't be true. Cold sweat formed on her body. I feel like throwing up. Stay calm. Breathe in. Breathe out. Repeat and stay fucking calm. Please.

"Make sure she won't get any kind of protection from them. Do everything you can to stop it." After listening to García, Luciano spoke again, "Yes, I know. You don't need to remind me. Put a number on it."

Nina wondered whether García had a good sense of humour because for some reason, Luciano smiled. Granted, it looked more like a baring of teeth than a smile.

"Fine." He lowered the phone from his ear.

"Marietta doesn't know anything," Severino said.

Severino's initial response was extremely telling of their relationship in Nina's opinion. She read a semblance of disgust and disdain on expression while his eyes appeared indifferent.

"She might know more than she let on," Luciano argued.

"Why were you laughing?" she couldn't help but ask Luciano.

"When did I laugh?" He arched a brow.

"You know what I mean," she said with gritted teeth and a sweet smile. "Shortly before you hung up. You smiled – very widely if I might add."

"You don't want to know. I know I don't."

34

CHAPTER 34

In the middle of the night, the argent moon was at its highest point and shone upon Nina's skin as if to highlight the sins on them. She looked at the hidden stars in the dark sky through the glass of the sunroom. Just because you couldn't see them, didn't mean they weren't there. No matter how many times Nina cleansed herself, her hands were still tainted.

Hitherto, it had been a hectic day. To be alone with her thoughts had her drumming her fingers against her elbows. She always liked to think she wasn't capable of such things. But here she was. The worst part were her conflicting views on her actions. A strange sense of comfort hid in nooks and crannies as she took in the sight of Luciano's shadowy figure in the garden.

He was making yet another phone call.

She had already told him to sit down and rest his leg, but he didn't listen. It was as if he couldn't bring himself to sit still for one second.

Since the French doors were open, Nina was able to hear him from time to time. Whilst vague, she had an idea what awaited them.

The aggressive ringing of the doorbell reached her ears. She walked to the front door, wondering who it was. The ringing returned just as she opened the door.

Nero? And here I thought it was going to be Severino.

"Nina," Nero said looking a bit stunned. "My apologies for the ringing. I was expecting Luciano to answer."

"He is here if you want to see him," she moved to the side so he would come inside.

Only now that he came closer to, Nina picked up on the repulsive smell coming off him – not that she showed it. He may have looked picture perfect but clearly, he hadn't showered yet. Whatever she smelled in the church was pleasant compared to this. The only guess she could take was that he had been busy burning bodies before burying their charred remains.

"Would you like to drink something?" she asked politely as they made their way to Luciano.

"No, thank you." He arched his dark-blonde brow at her question. "I apologise for threatening to shoot you," he said right before entering the sunroom.

"It's alright. I can see why you did what you did." She sent him her signature smile. Nina regarded him; it was crystal clear he wasn't sure what to say. "You should smile more, Nero."

"Why?"

"Why? Shouldn't you be happy I haven't told Luciano about it?"

Nina noticed how he immediately checked if Luciano heard her before settling his eyes on her.

Yet. Should I say it? No, I might give him a heart attack if I did. He looks worn down as is. He deserves it for pointing that damned gun at me though.

"I deserve that. Thank you," Nero said with a strained smile. "Good night, Nina."

"Good night."

Nina returned to her previous spot. Their conversation appeared to be going smoothly until she saw Nero gripping his dirty-blonde hair. A few words coming out of their mouths travelled to her, bringing about a quiet sob that she quickly tried to suffocate.

So I didn't mishear it earlier.

She got up and left, hoping for the shadows inside the mansion to hide her crestfallen visage. Without realizing it, she began frowning at herself. As the wife of a notorious gangster, it was only to be expected that he'd go to prison one day. It was only sooner than expected.

The price Luciano had to pay García wasn't a stack of cash like it usually was. The Bureau wanted to get their hands on a big fish for a long time now and García would be the man to give it to them on a silver platter, ensuring a boost in his career.

After mentally slapping herself on the wrist, Nina dried the tears off her cheeks.

Maybe it's not for that long. I can hope, can't I?

Nausea hit Nina all of a sudden. She ran to the bathroom and emptied the little contents inside her stomach. She breathed onto her palm and got a whiff of her breath.

Not that bad – compared to Nero.

Not wanting anyone to see her like this, she went upstairs to brush her teeth. There was no need for Luciano to worry about her. She believed he already had too much on his mind. After rinsing her mouth one last time, she returned downstairs.

The touch of a familiar hand had Nina's still for a second before she turned around. She forgot her husband had golden ears.

"You heard?" Luciano asked to which she lightly nodded her head.

He must have noticed the change in her complexion. The feel of his palm against her left cheek made Nina want to look away, afraid that the windows to her soul would give away too much.

Knowing what he was about to ask, she said, "I'm fine."

"Why won't you let me worry about you?"

She could feel her eyes welling up. He was still in front of her, touching her, talking to her, yet it felt like he was made of smoke. For how much longer would he be there? A lone tear pearled down her flushed cheek.

"Silly girl," he chuckled before wiping her tear away.

"It's not funny." She looked him dead in the eyes.

"We'll make the best of it."

"For how long?"

"Give or take a few years. Nothing is set in stone so I can't say for sure."

"Can we sit down for a minute?" Her legs felt like giving out.

"Sure."

They went back to the sunroom, the fresh air acting as a balm to Nina's frayed mind. While Luciano stretched his injured leg on the couch, Nina only took up the edge.

Her body was turned to him, her fingers delicately reaching out to his leg. "How is it?"

"Could be worse."

"Do you know what you're charged with?"

"In the grand scheme of things, it's all very minor stuff. Battery is going to be one of them for sure." He laughed quietly to himself. "Not that I needed García to help with that one; I have myself to thank for that one," he said as he grabbed her hand, mindlessly playing with the marquise cut diamond of her wedding ring.

That's not that bad. Nina sighed in relief.

"What else?"

"Do you want to take a guess?"

"You're really taking this in stride, aren't you?"

"It's not my first time doing time, Nina."

"Really?"

His lips twitched at her surprise. "I was much younger, so I got away with a lot and I'm pretty sure my father had in hand in an early release." He sobered up. "García told me the other charge will have something to do with the horse races – match-fixing, drugging et cetera. We'll have to see."

"What about everything that happened at the church?"

"We covered our steps. Nero made sure of it. Even if they do ever find evidence, we'll have another unfortunate soul take the fall for it."

Nina merely nodded. A sardonic smile playing on her lips as she imagined someone's paying for her crimes. Grace began slipping through her fingers like sand, or maybe it had already begun the second she was born into the Sciacca household.

"Who?" She wanted to know who would pay for her sins.

"Having a conscious won't do you any good, Nina." Luciano held her by the nape so she would look at him.

"Who?" She pressed.

"Someone who'll deserve it." He caressed the side of her neck with his knuckles. "If you want, it could be someone who arranges dog fights or races? I know of a few who could take the fall for us."

"Willingly?"

"More or less."

Luciano dropped his hand, leaving Nina cold. She reached out to him, wanting him to caress her, hold her or simply have his hand rested on her thigh. Anything to not be separated.

"It's cold," she said.

"Turn around," Luciano said and pulled her against him when she did so. "Still cold?" He wrapped his muscled arm around her waist after moving all of her hair to one side.

She laughed a little. "No."

"You can close your eyes," he mumbled against her shoulder.

"Why would I want to do that?"

"I don't know about you, but that's how I fall asleep."

"I don't want to," her voice softer than before.

"Why is that?" He drew calming circles on her waist.

"If I fall asleep here, who is going to take me to bed? You? With your injury? I'm not that cruel."

"I'd manage." Luciano chuckled. "Afraid of nightmares?"

She meekly shood her head. "No. Afraid that I won't."

Luciano tensed; his hand stopped drawing circles before sliding his eyes to her. "You think you can afford to have something like that weighing on your conscious? Be happy that it doesn't."

"Does it ever weigh on you?"

"I don't give it much thought. I prefer having one of them dead than one of us."

"Can't afford to," she echoed after him. She hummed in agreement then said, "I think I'll do that."

35

EPILOGUE

Dark, heavy clouds hung low over the city and the sight made Luciano feel at ease somehow, the crackling of the fireplace adding to it. His uncle, Affonso, sat before him, waiting for Luciano to start a conversation that was long overdue. Luciano played with the white queen on the chessboard, twirling it between his fingers. When heavy rain hit the window to his right, he put the piece down.

"I don't want you to just take over as acting don," Luciano finally said to Affonso. "I'll step down and you'll be the don."

Affonso raised a sceptical eyebrow. "Is this about you going behind bars?"

"Yes."

"You think you can't be the don when you're in prison?" Affonso smirked. "Your father did it."

"I know, but it's not the same. I'm new and young. The Outfit needs stability. I want business to be run effectively. Me being in prison will slow things down."

"You're more pragmatic than I thought." Affonso chuckled in surprise. "When you get out, you'll get your place back. You have my word," he promised before shaking hands on it with Luciano.

"I know you can handle it," Luciano spoke with certainty.

Affonso leaned back, eyeing his nephew with a wry gin. "You don't have to butter me up. We already agreed on it."

Luciano laughed with a nodding of the head. "That's true, but that doesn't mean I don't appreciate the way you handle things."

The Victorian style mansion of Nicolò greeted Luciano and Nina as they came through the tall gates. Once at the door, they rang the bell and one of the maids answered their call.

"Good morning. Where is my grandfather?" Luciano questioned the maid as he walked past her and inside the mansion.

"He is with your brother, Sir. Upstairs and third room on your left."

They thanked the maid and ascended the stairs, following her instructions. After a brisk knock, Luciano opened the bedroom's door. In front of them laid Teodoro's bandaged figure with Nicolò sitting at his side.

"You two came early," Nicolò said as he got up from the chair.

"I don't blame them. Who wouldn't want to be around this pretty face all day long?" Teodoro winked at his brother and sister-in-law.

Luciano rolled his eyes. "Would it kill you to be humble?"

Nina greeted Nicolò with kisses on the cheeks. "How are you, Nonno?"

"Come here, Nina." Nicolò lifted his cane off the floor and hugged her. "I've been told what you have done for my boys. Thank you," He spoke in a low volume so only she could hear him. He was beholden to her.

Overcome with emotion, Nina only moved to meet his gaze and smiled at him since she thought her voice wouldn't be stable. Suddenly, a roaring laugh followed by loud coughs echoed the room, making them look at Teodoro.

"She went to the police?" Teodoro let his head fall on the cushion.

"Yes," Luciano said begrudgingly.

"Damn whore," Teodoro muttered. "I never liked her to begin with."

"You don't say," sarcasm laced Luciano's voice.

"So what? Getting Banion to get us killed wasn't enough? She wanted to have our corpses behind bars on top of that? This woman has a penchant for drama," Teodoro said.

"It's not impossible for Marietta to have tipped them off but-" Luciano began.

"It's unlikely," Nicolò chimed in.

Teodoro's grey eyes landed on Nina, glistening with mischief which had Nina mentally sighing. "Maybe you should be the one to take care of her."

"I think I'll pass on the offer," Nina said.

"She's alright, Luciano," Teodoro grinned from ear to ear. "You have my blessing for this union of yours."

Nina rolled her eyes at him. "If I had known you were doing this well, I wouldn't have come."

"Make that we," Luciano added.

"Sure, tell that to yourself. Whatever helps you guys sleep at night," Teodoro drawled.

Dawn came and it was time for Nina and Luciano to end their visit. After saying their goodbyes, they drove past the closing iron gates and navigated the roads of Lincoln Park.

"I've assigned another bodyguard to you," Luciano said.

"What?" hints of irritation leaked into Nina's tone.

"Another one in addition to Bartolomeo," he clarified.

The only reason why Luciano decided on keeping Bartolomeo was because Nina might prefer having faces she knew at home. After all, he wouldn't be around for much longer.

Once they neared their home, Nina caught a glimpse of Nero's blonde hair as he stood right by the gates. The forbidding expression on him had her heart sinking into an abyss. These moments of mental collapse were endless lately.

Luciano pulled up and rolled Nina's window down allowing Nero to speak.

"Leave everything on your body in the car before you get out. Enrique is here," Nero gritted out.

"Already?" Nina's voice turned to stone.

"Apparently. I think Enrique couldn't wait to get his hands on our don."

"Affonso is your don now," Luciano said calmly before signing Nero to step back from the vehicle.

An ungracefully tall and thin man entered Nina's vision. That must be him, she thought. The air around him flipped like a coin the second he saw Luciano. While Nina kept appearances up, the man made her feel uneasy. García spared no seconds to make his move as Luciano and Nina got out of the car.

"I don't believe we've met. It's a pleasure to meet you." García abruptly shook Nina's hand.

Fuck off. You're even nauseating to look at.

"Pleasure is all mine." Nina forced a smile.

"I was hoping for this to go as peacefully as possible," Enrique García said to Luciano whilst wearing the smile of a snake on his lips.

"I'd like a moment with my wife before we continue." Luciano placed his hand on Nina's back, leading them away from the crooked agent. He turned his head toward him, then asked, "If that's alright with you?"

"Of course! I'll be waiting in the car." He did a little wave of the hand at them.

"What happens now?" Nero asked Luciano while his eyes stayed on García.

"I've already given out orders for loose ends." Luciano went in for a hug from his cousin. "You and Nina will have to tell the rest where I am."

"Take care." Nero hit him on the back before stepping away and giving them some privacy.

The precious brown eyes of his wife brimmed with tears. One spilled over leading Luciano to kiss it away. "I'm willing to bet I haven't even seen all of it."

"You'd win that bet." She laughed softly. "I don't want you to go, Luciano" her voice wavered.

He tightly embraced her one last time. "You have no idea how happy you make me feel by just saying that." He lightly touched her silk hair, committing all of her to his memory. Then, without a word, he slipped his wedding ring off his finger and dropped it onto Nina's palm. "Hold onto this for me."

She let her tears fall freely, nodding before sliding it onto her own ring finger. "It's too big."

"Obviously." He arched a brow at her. "I thought you were bright, but I'm not so sure anymore."

She laughed softly, taking the golden band off her finger. "I think I'll wear it as a necklace."

There she was laughing and crying at the same time. Luciano thought her to be a sight for sore eyes. "I'll come back to you," he promised while cradling her head, pressing his forehead against hers.

A small smile formed onto her lips. The way he held her reminded her of their time in the garden. She held onto the good memory, wanting to send him off with a smile rather than tears. "I'll be waiting for you."

www.ingramcontent.com/pod-product-compliance
Lightning Source LLC
Chambersburg PA
CBHW070921190726
48292CB00004B/1053